TALES PLAYER:

The Melodious Journeys of a Space Faring Band

By Shawn P. Madison

Copyright© 2022 Shawn P. Madison
ISBN: 978-81-8253-928-0

First Edition: 2022
Rs. 200/-

Cyberwit.net
HIG 45 Kaushambi Kunj, Kalindipuram
Allahabad - 211011 (U.P.) India
http://www.cyberwit.net
Tel: +(91) 9415091004
E-mail: info@cyberwit.net

Dedicated to Steve Mazey, who not only gave me the original idea for The Player but also enjoyed the stories enough to give them their very first publication. My many thanks to you, Steve.

Contents

Everybody in the Whole Cellblock 5
Only Fools Rush In 11
Caught In A Trap 35
You Ain't Never Caught A Rabbit 69
A Little Less Conversation 101

Everybody in the Whole Cellblock

Another small explosion rocked the courtyard, spraying rocks and smaller chunks of asphalt down on the panicked crowd. Everywhere she looked, people in uniform ran for cover or to retrieve weapons from the arsenal on the other side of the great open space.

What just minutes before had been a concert for the various military personnel stationed in the adjacent Tenafore Outpost and the inmate population of the renowned Tenafore Penitentiary had turned into a bloody melee of screams and discharging weapons – to what purpose, Red Alonzo had no clue.

What she did have a clue about was how to run and she was doing a damn good job of that right now, her vid-tech close on her heels. Reporting on the concert for the UEN Military Entertainment Network should have been an easy assignment. Instead, with her arms covering her face and head, she ran as far from the latest set of explosions as she could, wondering if she would survive the night.

A great boom rocked the courtyard and Red found herself stumbling across the rubble strewn asphalt, skidding to a halt against the inner wall of the amphitheater. Benji Jensen ended up sliding over her with a grunt and a gasp, the wind having been knocked out of him by his collision with the low wall.

Raising her head to get a better look at the situation, she saw dozens of soldiers charging in all directions, as well as the orange jumpsuited prisoners scrambling for cover. But through all of that, through a hazy veil of dust and debris still settling down on the huge area, she thought she could see several members of the band, who had just been up on stage, engaging with the attacking enemy.

A short man with black hair, who seemed to have been directing the pyrotechnic displays for the band before all this started, had just launched what looked to be a rocket at a small launch vehicle, already listing to the left on the ground about thirty-five meters away. His formerly black jacket was covered in dust and debris and through a fit of coughing he was loading another one of his pyro-technic rockets into a launch tube.

Another man, who had just been on stage playing amazing music with the band, was engaged in combat with a black clad enemy who had exited the fallen launch vehicle, quickly disarming the man and knocking him out cold with a hard chop to the back of the neck. Picking up the fallen enemy's weapon, he began pouring fire into what was left of the launch vehicle and was rewarded with a series of small explosions from the engines at the rear of the craft.

The tallest member of the band, the one who had been singing lead vocals, was still on stage engaged in a very animated conversation with what looked to be a high-ranking military officer, pointing toward yet another small launch vehicle still swooping down toward the courtyard.

Before she could swing her eyes back toward the small man with the black hair, he launched his rocket toward the incoming shuttle and another explosion rocked the space. With pieces of the ship crashing to the ground and still smaller bits pinging all around them, what was left of the vehicle's lift suddenly gave out and it began a very slow plummet toward the surface.

In a hail of more small rocks and bits of concrete, Red got her legs out from under her, yanked on Benji's collar and got them both moving again. Soldiers began streaming back into the area from the arsenal, now heavily armed, and searching for those who had infiltrated the crowd and started this mess about six minutes ago.

The shuttle that had just been damaged swirled out of control and slammed into the asphalt about fifty yards away, in the opposite direction from the stage than its also doomed companion ship. The whine of the shuttle's engines, still engaged but sounding erratic, added to her anxiety level as she huffed her way toward the exit of the open-air amphitheater and what she hoped was safety.

"What in the hell is going on here?" Jensen managed to rasp between coughs but Red had no breath to spare for an answer. They entered a dark tunnel with light showing at the opposite end but it was far too crowded with panicked prisoners and Penitentiary Guards trying to herd and control them.

"Not this way," she shouted above the concentrated volume of so many panicked voices and yanked Benji in a new direction. Here there was another man who she remembered was with the band during her pre-concert interview – although with multiple bleeding cuts and a large gash in his left forearm, he was providing first aid to a soldier who had been injured in the initial attack.

Looking her way, he told her that everything was going to be all right as it was nearly over now. She shook her head to clear the ringing and saw how calmly he was dressing the soldier's leg wound. Glancing up at her again, he motioned with his eyes toward the down shuttles and the stage. "See," he said and coughed. "My guys and the military have it all under control."

"Your guys?" she questioned and he laughed, turning back to the man he was ministering first aid to.

Looking back over her shoulder Red could see the former battlefield had visibly calmed. Soldiers were no longer running but instead were performing search patterns throughout the courtyard, trying to identify any additional attackers. Several of the musicians were back on the stage, dusting off their instruments and checking their equipment. Smoke from the ruined shuttles, which had been thick just moments earlier, was clearly lessening as firefighters from the adjacent base sprayed them with mobile foam packs. Many men dressed in black were lying facedown on the ground, wire cuffs securing their wrists tightly behind their backs. Their not so lucky comrades were being piled up in an orderly line, at least a dozen so far, their now sightless eyes pointing toward the night sky.

Max Gun'Jhur rocked back on his heels as medics came, scooped up the wounded soldier and whisked him away. Standing next to Red, he slowly looked around at the carnage that covered the immediate area. He put a hand on Benji Jensen's shoulder to steady the clearly shell-shocked vid-tech and took a deep breath before coughing again.

Red looked at him, clearly confused, and asked again, "Your guys?"

Max let out a small laugh then and smiled at her. "We've been in situations like this before, unfortunately…"

"Your band, those musicians," and Red pointed toward the stage where all members of the band seemed to be back in their positions, "have all been in battle before?"

"Oh, if you only knew, Ms. Alonzo," Max said. "If you only knew…"

Just then the lead singer, known throughout known space as The Player, walked up to the microphone and cleared his throat. Red listened as he thanked the men and women of the military base for their assistance in thwarting the attempted jailbreak that had just transpired. It seemed that the Russian Oligarch who was meant to be freed, a former high-ranking member of an organized criminal element from the lower grids, had also died during the defensive maneuvers that blocked the attacking party's plan. A huge wail of applause erupted from the hundreds of soldiers crowded into the space and she could see the man called Max smiling next to her.

Turning toward Benji Jensen, she whispered, "You're getting all this, right?"

Jensen merely nodded and pointed to the green lights on the rig that covered his back and wrapped around his chest. It was a testament to the manufacturer that the Vid-Tech equipment had survived his tumble to the hard ground and collision with the wall just a few minutes ago.

"Good…" she mumbled. "Good…"

The Player shouted for the small group of prisoners who had been in attendance before all of the action started to be brought back in to the amphitheater and while that was taking place he kept the crowd in rapt attention, reveling them with tales of other such skirmishes he and his band had been involved in. The crowd laughed and shouted back at him at all the right moments and, just like that, he had everyone calmed down and ready to have fun again.

"It's what he does," Max said as he wrapped a gauze bandage around the gash in his arm and fixed Red with a smile. "He's the best there is…"

Red found herself agreeing and smiled back at the handsome Max with a look of wonder in her eyes.

"You'll have to tell me more about all that sometime," she said to him. "Sounds like there's a great story there."

"You have my word, Ms. Alonzo," Max said and reached out to steady the still wobbly Jensen again. "You have my word."

The crowd suddenly hushed as the band went silent and the man known as The Player stood motionless at the microphone stand in the center of the stage. A throwback from an earlier time, it was just for show as the sound system was more than capable of carrying his voice and the band's music throughout the great open space without the prop.

Still, it made the concert a bit more nostalgic for the members of the audience. All eyes were on the singer as he scanned the crowd and the myriad faces, men and women of all races and religions who were willing to lay down their lives to protect everyone else.

"You know, I had another set planned for this concert, my friends," he said. "But in lieu of recent events…" the crowd chuckled. "I think I'll start off this time with something a little bit more uptempo than usual."

After the applause and cheers died down, The Player took in the crowd with a playful gleam in his eye.

"So, get ready now," he said. "Everybody…let's rock!"

Red listened as the band launched into a raucous song about a party in a county jail and a whole cell block of prisoners dancing. She loved it and it was pretty clear that the crowd did, too.

"So, when can we have that talk, Max?" Red asked, having to shout to be heard.

"Soon, Ms Alonzo," Max Ghun'Jur shouted back. "For now, just enjoy the show. Afterwards, we'll grab a bite to eat and a drink at a bar in the base next door and I'll fill you in on some of the band's exploits."

Only Fools Rush In

Soft music wafted its way through the dark caverns of Corpura Starport's grimy underbelly. Through a maze of confusing crossways, smoky corridors and filthy power junctions, the melody worked to soothe the many thousands of wayward travelers waiting for their turn to get off-planet.

An often hopeless cause, to say the least, but this tune was something uncommon in this region of Corpura's forgotten masses. A thing not so easily ignored or discarded but something to latch on to, something to be held closely, to be breathed in.

He passed row after row of the homeless and trapped, their heads slowly bobbing to the beat and the marvelous verse. It never ceased to amaze him how the music of this single player could infuse a sense of hope, of something better, into the lives of those with less than nothing to hold on to. Truly amazing...

But time was short. Max didn't plan on spending one scant second more than was absolutely necessary in this filthy stinking cavern. He was probably more than fifty levels below the surface at this point and the luxury liner Donello was leaving in about an hour. He'd been following the unmistakable beauty of the music, the rich tones of the rhythm, for quite some time now and could tell that he was closing in.

Max felt himself walking in step with the music, letting the smooth tones drive him forward through the thickening sprawl of Corpura's below-dwellers, ever closer to the man who was orchestrating the tune.

Trying not to inhale the stench of those he passed, Max turned a dark corner and felt the music become stronger. It enveloped him, it was much closer now, almost tangible. This was what he loved about the playing, the magic realism of the tunes and the soft tones of the verse being scarcely uttered by an almost mystical voice.

"God, he's good," Max mumbled to himself and then gasped as he caught a whiff of something awful emanating from the unidentifiable lump he had just stepped over. "Better than ever and anyone else in the business..." he continued.

Up ahead, in the barely lit shadows of a maintenance trunk, he finally caught sight of the musician and immediately stopped moving forward without realizing it, letting the music soak into his soul.

The acoustic guitar, a rare instrument in this day and age, was softly strumming, its gorgeous beat reverberating off the many walls in this cavernous maze.

"Hurry on, Max," he whispered to himself then, and once again began walking forward. Six strings and a single voice, simply remarkable. Max thought to himself, *How could it be possible that this one man could create such joy?*

Out of respect for the mesmerizing wave of sound being bestowed upon these hopeless thousands, Max stopped about a meter away from the musician and waited until he was noticed by the tall man.

We're leaving, he mouthed and the musician nodded once in understanding, slowly beginning to bring his song to an end. As the last guitar strum died away, fleeing like a lost memory into the depths of Corpura, there was a smattering of applause that seemed to come from all directions at once and then all was quiet.

The tall man slung the guitar over his right shoulder and walked past Max saying only two words, softly spoken in passing and almost missed, "Where to?"

"Martensburgengrad. It's on the outskirts of the Siberi Vastness."

The tall man stopped and turned to look at his manager. "Russian territory?"

"Not exactly," Max muttered and urged his friend forward. "But almost. Nothing to worry about, though, it's on the U.E.N. side of the border," he offered, walking double-time to keep up with the long-legged musician. "I booked you as the Primo Guest Entertainer on the luxury cruiser Donello—three sets a night, six nights."

"How about the band?"

"They're already aboard," Max sneered. "You're the only one I couldn't locate."

"Well, you're here aren't you?"

"By luck only," Max said and gestured to the hordes of people littering the dark caverns they were traversing. "It was a miracle that I found you, a sheer miracle."

The tall musician smirked and smiled at some of those people laying in the filth of Corpura's subterranean society. "It's all about the people, Max," he said with a smile on his lips. "Don't ever forget that it's all about the people."

*   *   *

The enormous luxury liner Donello, newly off the docks of the moon-based Luftwaffe Shipyards, moved swiftly through space using the recently perfected and improved interstellar drive first conceived of by the now legendary Sir Walter Blemeth on Earth in 2053. When the Grid-Division Treaty of 2100 had been signed just twenty-eight short e-years ago, nearly all of Earth's population took to the stars in order to avoid what would have surely been a cataclysmic war between the two global superpowers. The people of the United Earthian Nations had chosen the Upper Grid-Levels of Space to colonize while the United Soviet States had chosen the Lower Grids.

Although the idea was to avoid war by ceasing all contact between the two nations, it was inevitable that certain systems along either side of the border would be visited from time to time by people of the so-called 'other side.' It was astonishing, however, how very infrequently such crossings of the border actually occurred. Especially since there was no clear-cut line through space letting the people of each nation know exactly where they might be crossing the border while hurtling through the vacuum at speeds previously thought unattainable.

Needless to say, when such border crossings took place and were detected, being from the 'other side' could very likely get a person killed or a ship destroyed, and quickly at that.

For this reason, most interstellar travelers chose to fastidiously avoid the border between the two superpowers and an area of thousands of kilometers around it when going to wherever it was they were going to.

The Donello, on the other hand, was heading right for it. Or, to be more precise, to Martensburgengrad, a small planet in a system settled by U.E.N. citizens of mostly Soviet descent some three e-years ago. Eager to remain members of the U.E.N. and all that the great nation stood for, they were also eager to remain close to those people that they considered their family, their blood. Hence the location of Martensburgengrad so very close to the invisible line in space referred to simply as The Border.

A mere three hundred million kilometers from the Donello's destination lay the Siberi-Vastness and the territory of the United Soviet States. It was an imposing set of circumstances to be in, Maximillian Gun'jhur thought to himself, as he let his mind wander amidst the amazing set that was being played by the band now up on stage, known today by a new name—Johnny Vagabond and The Jazz Players.

Of course, the U.E.N. Military heavily patrolled the billions and billions of kilometers of border shared by the two superpowers on a routine basis but, knowing just how sparse the U.E.N. Fleet was in comparison to the sheer amount of space to be covered only served to spike Max's nervousness and take it up a notch.

"Thank God for the music," he snickered to himself and a young man pressed up to him at the bar in the crowded auditorium that was the Donello's Recreation Center nodded and thanked God in return.

Max laughed at that and was happy to see so many people all in one place falling in love with the music of the band. Then again, the music was inspired by just the one man, the tall musician playing lead guitar and singing lead vocals...

"I saw these guys playing on a quick jumper from Earth to Neptune one time," the same man leaned over to the girl in front of him and said, "Just a spur of the moment jam session, it was utterly amazing...they were called the Melancholy Blues Band back then."

"No way, buddy," the good looking lady said and shook her head. "I've seen these guys on Alpha Prime, they're called Gideon G. and The Sonic Breeze."

"You're both wrong," a newcomer chimed in. "That's Melodious Tunes up there."

"Actually," Max spoke up, feeling a little bit more free with his tongue due to the two or three glassfuls of blue tinted alcohol he'd recently sucked down his throat. "You're all three absolutely correct."

"What the hell are you talking about?" the girl asked, still dancing in place to the music.

"You've all heard this music before but under different names and being played by different bands," Max continued. "The only thing that is constant throughout is the man with the amazing voice playing lead guitar. He also goes by the illustrious name of The Player, perhaps you've heard of him?"

"No way, man," another young woman said from Max's right. "That can't be The Player up there, I heard he was clear across U.E.N. space playing in some new system this week. I'd love to see that guy."

"Change of plans, sweetheart," Max said and gave the pretty young woman his best smile. After she smiled in return, he decided to go on with his tale. "When he plays with the band, they often go by different names as they travel. Sometimes they call themselves Toby Lit and The Nomads, or maybe you've caught wind of Tall -T and The Wayfarers? All one and the same, sometimes a few of the key band-members will change, but there's only one person who holds it all together."

"Oh yeah, and how do you know so much," the cute little redhead to his right said, nudging him in the side with her elbow.

"Because, my friends," Max began, "You are looking at the manager of those musicians up there, the one person who recognized their raw musical talent and potential to become legendary." Max paused then for effect and also because he felt just a little bit woozy. "Maximillian Gun'jhur at your service, ladies and gentleman, and up there on that stage I present to you the one and only, the interstellarly famous, Tobias Thibodeau...better known throughout the Upper-Grid Levels of Space by two words and two words only. Your entertainer, the man who is making you all feel so good right now. Simply put...The Player."

* * *

Toby was having a great set, the music was flowing just right, his fellow band mates were all in synch and the crowd was ecstatic. On top of it all, he felt good, this was what he loved to do. Play music and sing his songs and make thousands of people happy.

He had to hand it to Max on this one, this gig was by far the best they'd had in quite some time. The cruiser was state of the art, their cabins larger than the few apartments he kept in key locations throughout the Upper-Grid Levels of Space, and the pay was outstanding. With any luck, if all their sets went this smoothly on the ride back to Corpura, he wouldn't mind being re-booked on the Donello every once in a while.

Just then he felt it, his body always in tune to the ways and means of the machine he was traveling in. Although no one in the crowd seemed to notice, he knew immediately that the big ship had cut its engines and was decelerating rapidly. A quick glance toward several of his band members proved that he was not alone with this knowledge.

Much to their credit, though, they didn't miss a beat and the song played out until the end. The applause was deafening and, for the moment, he forgot about the fact that the cruiser had just come to an unexpected and unscheduled stop and allowed himself to soak up the warmth and gratitude of the crowd. After many bows and gestures toward the members of his band, Toby announced that they were taking a quick break and would be back in five.

His eyes quickly searched the crowd for Max and found him in a far corner talking worriedly with a member of the Donello's crew. In seconds, Toby was moving through the crowd amidst a plethora of happy people, zeroing in on Max.

The band's manager caught sight of him, ended the conversation with the crewman and began to work his way toward the stage. Toby met him in the middle and Max led him back to the stage by the elbow. Not a word was exchanged during the short trip but as soon as they were back on stage Max turned to face him and Toby knew there was trouble.

"What is it, Max?"

"Well, Tobias," Max said and glanced nervously around at the other musicians who had gathered behind their lead singer. "A small Attack-Class Soviet warship hailed the captain several minutes ago and demanded that the ship come to a full stop. The crew thinks that they plan on boarding us, for what reason remains unknown."

"Soviets," Toby sighed and shook his head in amazement. "I knew this gig was too good to be true."

"Don't worry, Tobias," Max assured him. "I'm sure that it's just a routine matter, nothing to worry about."

"Sure, Max," Toby smirked. "On the U.E.N. side of the border, a Soviet military vessel demands to board us and it's simply routine."

Max shrugged then and gave in to common sense. Something was wrong, he knew it and Toby knew it. Hell, half the band knew it as soon as they sensed the ship's engines slowing down. Most of them were engineers in their prior lives, Toby almost insisted on playing alongside musicians who had been involved in engineering at one time or another as a matter of course. Engineering, Toby felt, was the key to musical perfection. When you understood mathematics and the ways in which the universe operated at the quantum level, then music was simple and pure. Toby wouldn't have it any other way.

"What's the captain going to do?" Tobias Thibodeau asked his manager.

"What else?" Max responded. "Let them come aboard."

Toby took a deep breath and looked at the members of his band. "This is going to be a long day, boys and girls."

* * *

"You tell your commander," Captain Adelson of the Donello said gruffly to the Soviet interpreter standing on his bridge. "That this ship is not his property nor the property of the United Soviet States and will not be crossing that border into Russian territory unless my dead body is lying on the deck of this bridge first."

The interpreter stared hard at Adelson for several seconds and then relayed the message to his commander. The face of the tall man standing next to the interpreter turned dark red as the message was translated into his native tongue. His uniform made it more than obvious that he was in charge of the Soviet soldiers standing on the Donello's bridge and Adelson saw the man's right hand start to twitch and move toward his holstered blaster. If there was an example to be made to the men of the Donello's crew, Adelson knew that he would be that example. *Better to end up dead than to endure any imprisonment in a Soviet gulag,* he thought to himself and began to make peace with his creator.

The Soviet commander took a single step forward and peered down into Adelson's eyes. He barked something quickly in Russian and the interpreter smirked.

"My commander says that this can be arranged very easily if you are not careful," the interpreter stated and his commander continued in Russian.

Adelson looked over at the interpreter, who had remained silent after the commander's remarks, and made an impatient gesture, "Will you translate that, interpreter? Or was it some sort of feeble Russian joke?"

The smile disappeared from the interpreter's face and he glanced nervously at his commander. In a subdued voice, the interpreter looked back at Adelson and said in perfect English, "My friend, this is not the time to make light of your circumstances. My commander does not tolerate such behavior by his own men and will definitely not tolerate it from his prisoners. I suggest you cooperate fully if you expect to remain alive."

Adelson wasn't looking at the interpreter, instead staring straight up and into the eyes of the Soviet commander. "You can tell him exactly what I said, interpreter, including the following—being the cowardly dogs that you are, as I am sure all Soviets are, I do not expect to remain alive after the next few minutes. Scum such as yourself, and do make sure that you translate the word 'scum' precisely, board my vessel with weapons waving against innocent citizens of the U.E.N., all too obviously with the intent of stealing this ship and taking it across the border back into your space. Why should I expect you to keep any of us alive unless, of course, it is to serve as slaves in one of your renowned prison camps. Cowards like you have no place in this universe, you should all be eradicated and I can not wait for the U.E.N. military to show up in this system and blow your sorry asses to hell and back."

The translator took in a deep breath and glanced nervously at his commander again.

"Tell him, interpreter," Adelson growled and one of the Donello's crewmen mumbled that he should keep himself quiet.

"Whatever happens, Blanton," Adelson said to his First Officer. "Cooperate fully with these people."

"They are going to kill you, Captain, if you continue to speak this way," Blanton muttered and was nudged in the side by a charger-wielding Soviet soldier.

"I know," Adelson said and sighed. "But if speaking in this way to this coward's face gets me fried a little quicker than the rest of you, I think it's well worth it. The Soviets will either kill everyone aboard this vessel or they will very likely take everyone into their space as prisoners. I, for one, do not wish to live one extra second in a Soviet prison."

The Soviet commander was listening to his interpreter with anger growing hot in his eyes. Adelson managed to tell Blanton one more time to cooperate before a single blaster bolt tore off his head.

Blanton watched in horror as Adelson's body slumped to the ground and suddenly, the attention was all on him.

"Tell your commander that we will cooperate fully with his demands, interpreter," Blanton muttered, hating himself as he said the words. He was just as patriotic as the next man, Blanton knew, but getting his head blown off at this very moment was not something Doug Blanton was ready for.

*　*　*

Tobias Thibodeau looked over the members of his band and felt confident in their abilities to survive this insanity. They had been able to discard their instruments on the stage and meld into the crowd before the first Soviet troops had shown up in the big ship's Recreation Center. There were several thousand of the Donello's passengers and crew stuffed into the large space and they were currently being addressed by a man in a Soviet uniform speaking English with absolutely no trace of an accent.

Looking into the eyes of his bass player and his keyboardist, Toby knew then exactly what they needed to do. The crew of the Donello had just lost their captain and had made the decision to cooperate fully with the invading Soviet forces. This meant one of two things for everyone on board—either death or a long and tortured existence as a Soviet prisoner. Neither one of those options appealed to Tobias Thibodeau at the current moment. He turned slightly toward Swayne Morrison, a miracle worker with a pseudo-synthesizer, and told him to take Rider Boone, his bass player, and get down to the engine room. The two engineers would more than know exactly what to do once they got there.

Turning to Max, Toby muttered, "I need a diversion, Max, and quickly."

"Right," Ghun'jur answered and began to work his way over to the stage. "Excuse me," he called out, interrupting the Soviet soldier's speech and motioning toward the equipment on the stage. "I need to begin taking the sound equipment offline before it gets overheated."

"You, come down from there and rejoin the crowd," the Soviet said and shifted his half-charger into a better firing position.

"Look, this equipment is quite fickle," Max said and turned several dials on two amps. "If they overload, it could be dangerous..."

"I will not repeat myself," the Soviet began.

"Too late!" Max called and jumped off the stage as both amps began to squeal in higher and higher decibels just before they exploded in a shower of sparks and small fireballs.

The crowd fell apart then and people began screaming and heading for the exits. The Soviets shouted above the din, trying to regain control, some brandishing weapons in their efforts to calm the stampeding mass of humanity down a bit.

Several seconds later it was clear that there would be no more fireworks out of the destroyed equipment and the crowd began to settle down. No one seemed to notice that Swayne and Rider had exited the large room during the brief melee. Tobias grinned at Max as he was being searched over by a rough Soviet soldier but, with a look of pure fright and confusion on his almost boyish features, as only Max could perfect, they soon let him go and he stumbled back over toward Toby.

"Good job," Thibodeau snickered.

"All in a day's work, Tobias," Max replied and let out a deep breath. "Let's just hope this works."

* * *

Freddie Natoki brought his left fist down hard at the base of the Soviet soldier's skull and the man quickly fell to the corridor's deck like so much deadweight. Relieving the soldier of his half-charger and blaster pistol, a nice little blue-black model like none he'd ever seen before, he pulled out two pair of duralloy cuffs and bound the unconscious man's wrists and ankles together.

Taking one quick glance around, the Donello's Chief of Security felt more confident now that he possessed weaponry similar to that of the invading forces. He had disabled four of the enemy soldiers already but had no idea just how many had originally boarded the gigantic luxury liner. Three of his fifteen member security detail had been killed by the Soviets so far, something that made him hate these Russian bastards all the more. Three good men...dead. They hadn't even been armed with anything more than sensor stunners, light crowd-control devices used to subdue the occasionally too-drunk guest aboard ship. Just their uniforms, that was all it had taken to cause their deaths. That and the fact that an example needed to be set for the rest of his detail. The twelve remaining security men had been split up then into four groups.

Incapacitating the man who had been guarding his party had been easy, almost too easy, but Freddie wasn't about to complain. He had immediately dispatched the two men with him to the Security HQ to try and find out more of exactly what was happening and to try and raise the alarm to the local U.E.N. Military Outpost. That had been more than an hour ago and he had not been able to raise those men on intra-ship com-link since.

Natoki heard the unmistakable sounds of several men trying to work their way covertly down the intersecting corridor and he froze as they approached. He was just about to lunge at them from around the corner with weapons blazing when he realized that they were not Soviet soldiers. Both men hit the deck hard anyway before he had a chance to stop his momentum. They were both lying there with wide eyes and staring at him as if he was death incarnate.

"What are you two up to?" he asked.

"We're going to the engine room," one of them muttered.

"Oh, you are?" Natoki questioned, still not certain of the intentions of these two.

"Yes, sir," the other quickly said and made his way slowly to his feet. "And if you're smart, you'll help us get there."

Natoki watched the other man as he gained his feet as well and recognized them both from the band of musicians who he had performed background checks on not too long ago. "Why would musicians need to get to the engine room?"

"Because we're engineers in real-life," Rider Boone said and awareness suddenly dawned on Fred Natoki's face.

"Then what are we waiting for, gentlemen?" Natoki said and led the way down the corridor. The engine room was just a few levels down and not very far away.

*   *   *

"Commander," a young technician called from his spot on the Donello's bridge. "I have a warning indicator on two of the four main engines."

"What is it? The instrumentation?" Commander Rugyev asked.

"No, sir, not as far as I can tell," the young man answered.

"Dammit," Rugyev barked and opened a channel to the Soviet warship floating not too very far away from the Donello's current position. "Captain Stonyenko, we have a problem in the engine room."

"How serious is it?" came the raspy reply in Russian. "Can you continue at present speed?"

"Unsure, Captain," Rugyev stated with obvious disappointment. "I will have the situation checked out immediately but we should stop at this time until the matter can be resolved."

"That is not wise, Commander," the captain's voice rang through with obvious concern. "Need I remind you that we are still not in Soviet space?"

"Not at all, Captain," Rugyev said. "But these indicators show two engines ready to overload. If that happens, this ship as well as our own would be destroyed at this range. I will make every effort to see that this situation is handled as promptly as possible."

"Please do, Rugyev," Stonyenko growled. "Despite the fact that we are jamming any transmissions coming from that monstrosity, our jamming also limits our ability to sight any approaching U.E.N. warships on long-range scanners. Am I clear?"

"Yes, sir," Rugyev answered quickly.

"Good then," Stonyenko's voice quipped. "Keep me posted."

Rugyev glared at the young tech overseeing the engine room readouts and called over to a small Asian man sitting at the communications console. "Tao Chi, go down to the engine room and find out what is causing these indicators to read in the red."

"Yes, Commander," Chi said and disappeared down the bridge access tunnel.

Rugyev watched him go and thought immediately of sabotage. But who? He thought that all the passengers and crew were accounted for. "Damn this act of stupidity!" He grumbled to himself more than to anyone else. *Why in all the Known Grid-Levels of Space would the powers-that-be want a captured U.E.N. luxury liner and the thousands of people aboard her...?*

* * *

Tobias Thibodeau felt a slight tug on his left sleeve and looked over to see Rider Boone at his left elbow.

"Fifteen minutes," Boone said in a very serious tone. "Not a second longer. Maybe a few seconds shorter."

Toby nodded and began to approach the Soviet soldier who seemed to be in charge. A large man with a dark complexion was following the same path as Toby, at a distance of about five meters. Thibodeau recognized him as the man who had re-entered the Recreation Center with Rider and Swayne. Max Ghun'jur was about two meters behind Tobias and to his right. A group of three Soviets immediately recognized their group approach and began to raise some very lethal looking weapons in a defensive posture.

"No, no," Tobias said and raised his arms above his head, declaring a position of non-confrontation. "We just need to talk, you and I."

"About what?" The Soviet soldier in the middle sneered.

"About the fact that this ship's engines are about to explode due to extreme stress and overload," Thibodeau explained. "An irreversible condition that will result in the deaths of everyone aboard this ship as well as the destruction of your own ship at this distance."

"And I should believe this because...?" the soldier prompted.

"Check with the bridge and your commander," Thibodeau suggested and set his attention on some imaginary grit caught underneath the fingernail of his left index finger. "They'll confirm that this ship's engines are red-lighting off the charts with no discernible cause."

"I will not waste my time on..." the soldier began but was cut off by the shrill alarm klaxon that sounded throughout the auditorium.

Right on time, Tobias laughed to himself and realized that the engines couldn't have reached such a critical stage at any better moment than just then. The Soviet soldier immediately walked over to a com-link panel set into the wall near the entrance to the oversized auditorium and held a brief yet excited conversation with someone on the Donello's bridge. Disconnecting the link, the man marched directly over to Thibodeau and poked him sternly in the chest. "What do you know about this?"

"Only that engine overload, once begun, is irreversible and will result in imminent destruction, as I explained before," Thibodeau said, barely glancing away from his fingernail as he spoke. The smaller Russian looked up into Thibodeau's eyes and raised his weapon, as did the other ten or so soldiers in the vast room.

"You did this!" He boomed and, suddenly, the only sound in the entire auditorium was the continuing shrill of the alarm klaxon.

Thibodeau looked down at the man and crossed his arms across his chest, trying to look utterly confident while his heart was pounding. "Of course," he said and glared into the man's eyes.

"Stop it now," the Soviet soldier said and tapped Thibodeau's chest with the muzzle of his half-charger.

"I told you twice already," Thibodeau said. "Irreversible. That means, for those of you who are too stupid to understand, no going back. No stopping it. Destruction. Boom. And it will take all of you with it as well."

"You would kill yourselves rather than be taken prisoner?" Another Soviet soldier asked from about four meters away.

"Absolutely..." Thibodeau said and saw the stunned reaction on the soldier's face.

"You are insane," the man in charge said and backed up a step or two from Tobias. "This is madness. All we want is the ship, no harm was to come to any of you."

"Tell that to the captain of this vessel," Thibodeau said and then snapped the fingers on his right hand. "Oh, that's right, you can't because you people killed him. And now, we'll return the favor and kill all of you."

"Not today," the Russian said and smiled. "Lock them all in here. By order of Commander Rugyev, we're leaving this deathtrap."

Thibodeau watched the Soviet soldiers quickly exit the Recreation Center with their weapons trained on the crowd as Max and Fred Natoki moved up to his side. Once the soldiers were gone and the hefty clank of the entrance hatch locks slammed into place, the room erupted with frantic questions, some screams and a plentitude of panic.

"Listen up, people!" Max shouted over the cries and the annoying braying of the alarm klaxon as he leaped on top of the stage and tried to gain control of the crowd. "Please do not panic, this situation is under control!"

"Is the ship going to explode?" A single question rose above all the shouting and the alarm.

"Well, yes and no," Max stumbled.

"What does that mean?" Someone else asked as the noise began to die down, although not the klaxon.

"It means that the engines are indeed rigged to blow up in about nine minutes," Max stated in a concerned tone. "But, it also means that we have a plan...a plan that we will put into action...or at least, I think we can put into action. However, first things first, we must all figure out a way to get those doors unlocked and we must be quick about it."

"Leave that to me," Fred Natoki said and produced the blue-black blaster of unfamiliar design from an ankle holster. Raising the weapon towards the thick doors of the recreation hall he smiled and said, "Stand back, everyone, this shouldn't take long."

* * *

Rugyev and his men ran down the corridor to the airlock where a shuttle was positioned to take he and his men back to the U.S.S. Stalingrad. All over the doomed luxury liner the alarm klaxon warned of impending destruction. Tao Chi, the engineer assigned to his boarding detail, had confirmed that several of the Donello's main engines had been rigged to overload beyond possibility of containment. It was the Obliteration Option, one of the oldest tactics in the military handbook, and he couldn't believe he had been taken in by it. Of course, he had not expected military tactics to surface from the crew-members of a non-military pleasure cruiser, but nevertheless, it was a standard ploy. One that had been used successfully for centuries, burn down the fortress rather than allow it to be captured. *Damn!* He chastised himself. *How could he have not seen it coming?*

Entering the large personnel transport's airlock, he secured a place for himself in the very front of the shuttle and watched dozens of his men quickly shuffle past to take their seats and begin to strap in for departure. It suddenly occurred to him that not all of them were leaving as had come aboard. Too late to figure out that mystery now, he knew, there were less than six minutes left before the Donello's engines were going to explode.

He felt the sudden rush of free-floating as the shuttle disengaged from the Donello's airlock and the big luxury liner quickly began to grow smaller in the large viewport in the shuttle's cockpit. *Damn them!*

"Will Captain Stonyenko destroy the ship before it blows, Commander?" One of his men asked from behind him.

"And waste one of our missiles on a doomed ship," Rugyev sneered. "I think not."

Faster, faster, Rugyev thought to himself. His shuttle needed to dock with the Stalingrad so that they could gain the necessary distance away from the doomed cruiser in order to avoid being destroyed themselves when the ship's massive engines blew. They were down to four minutes and counting when he felt the secure clang of metal on metal as their shuttle successfully docked with the small attack cruiser that he and his men called home. *Good riddance to you all*, he sighed inwardly. *May you all burn in hell...*

*   *   *

Rider Boone struggled with the panel on the massive engine's housing, sweat pouring freely down his face. He didn't only have Swayne Morrison as a back-up this time. The entire band was there in the engine room, pitching in, putting their engineering expertise to good use.

"Three minutes, Rider," Thibodeau said from the entrance to the engine room as he, Max and the Donello's First Officer, Doug Blanton, watched the men at work. "Will you be able to do this in time?"

"Only if you shut up for about the next two and a half minutes and let us do our job, here, boss," came Boone's strained reply.

"What will those Soviet pigs do when they realize that we aren't going to blow up?" Blanton asked.

Tobias turned to him and smiled. "Hopefully, we have that part covered."

"How's that?"

Thibodeau turned to Max Ghun'jur and said, "Are Martino and Gus in the escape pod terminal?"

"On the job and preparing all ten of the pods for immediate departure," Max confirmed.

Blanton stared at the two men with confusion on his face and Thibodeau realized that there was still some explaining left to do. "Two of my guys are working on the escape pods, matching targeting coordinates with those of the Soviet warship."

Blanton looked from Max to Tobias and back to Max again. "So?"

"So," Max continued with a toothy grin. "What most people don't realize is that escape pods have engines, too. Pretty powerful ones for such small ships. And when they are rigged to blow in close proximity to another vessel..."

"Let's just say," Thibodeau intervened. "A chain reaction of cosmic proportions often occurs."

* * *

"Ten seconds and counting, Captain," one of the Stalingrad's bridge crew stated as the Soviet warship struggled on standard thrust to put some distance between itself and the doomed U.E.N. luxury liner. Towing Rugyev's shuttle along prevented them from engaging their main engines but there had simply been no time to evacuate the shuttle and go to full burn. No need to worry, though, they had put more than enough space between the two vessels already.

"It's too bad, really," Stonyenko remarked to no one in particular. "The U.S.S. could have learned a lot from a ship of that size and speed. Too bad, really."

Just then, a sharp white light overtook the screen and a sharp streak flashed across the viewscreen where the Donello had been just moments before.

"It is done then?" Stonyenko asked aloud.

"It seems so, sir, but the sensor readings do not correlate," somebody answered from behind his command chair.

"Explain," Stonyenko ordered.

"There was indeed an explosion," the Soviet soldier began. "Powerful, yes, but not consistent with the type and size of the engines that were fitted to the Donello."

"Captain," another voice chimed in. "I have readings of several very small craft fast approaching our position!"

"What type of craft?"

"Readings indicate escape pods, sir," the man replied. "I count nine of them now, Captain, but there were ten of them at first. None of them show signs of life."

Awareness of the treachery being delivered upon him suddenly dawned on Stonyenko's face as he stood from his command chair and pounded his fist against his main console. "Disengage Rugyev's shuttle now! Engage main engines, evasive maneuvers, get this ship out of here!"

The bridge erupted in a mass of confusion and shouts as crewmembers scrambled to carry out Stonyenko's orders.

It is too late, Stonyenko thought as he heard that Rugyev's shuttle had been disengaged from the air-lock from one crewman and that the Stalingrad's main engines had come on line from another. *Those U.E.N. swine...*

All nine of the Donello's escape pods exploded simultaneously as they reached to within a hundred meters of the Stalingrad's hull. The explosion was fierce enough to penetrate the hull in several places, particularly just outside of the Stalingrad's engine room. Since the Soviet warship's main engines were just coming online at the moment of impact, they were that much more vulnerable to becoming overloaded. A situation which helped to accelerate their detonation.

The U.S.S. Stalingrad disappeared in a quick white flash that was vastly larger than that which had been created when the first of the Donello's escape pods exploded at the exact same instant that the luxury liner brought its two remaining engine mains on-line. The streak that Stonyenko had noticed as that pod had exploded was the Donello's rapid departure from the space surrounding the Stalingrad.

Rider Boone and Swayne Morrison had barely succeeded in shutting down the overload sequence they had started less than fifteen minutes earlier in two of the Donello's engine mains while Yivgeny Noel and Conor McCain, both wonderfully skilled musicians with the brass horns, had worked fastidiously to ensure that the remaining two engine mains, although cold, would start up smoothly and efficiently when needed.

Martino Velez and Gus Marilago, the band's two percussionists, had signaled the engine room with barely fifteen seconds to go that the escape pods had been programmed and were on their way.

* **

Tobias Thibodeau stood on the bridge with Max Ghun'jur, Doug Blanton, Fred Natoki and the remainder of the Donello's bridge crew. The readings from the ship's long-range scanners confirmed that the

U.S.S. Stalingrad had suffered a massive engine implosion and had been obliterated.

"Do you think they called for back-up before the end?" Ghun'jur asked nervously on the ship's small bridge.

"Not likely," Blanton replied, being careful not to stare at the corpse of his former captain lying on the deck not three meters away, covered with a nondescript white sheet. "They were jamming our transmissions ever since they showed up. That made it awfully hard for them to transmit out as well."

"Why did they even try this?" Max asked. "Don't they know that they could have started a war if something like this made the nets?"

"They had no fear this close to their border," Natoki stated in an even tone. "They were jamming our transmissions so there was no fear that we could get the word out. If they destroyed us, no one would ever know unless someone just happened to be performing a sensor scan in this area as they passed through and detected the residual radiation of our imploded engines. Even then, identifying the source of that radiation would be a hard task at best and identifying the cause of such an explosion would be even more difficult. They did not fear us because we were not a military vessel. They thought we were an easy target. I guess our band of traveling minstrels proved them wrong."

"Interesting," Ghun'jur said and let out a deep sigh. "But I still say that we put some distance between us and Martensburgengrad."

"No," Thibodeau said and stood up tall to his full height of better than two meters. "Go on toward your destination, First Officer. The Soviets will not send another ship this way until they find out exactly what happened to the Stalingrad. We're safe for now."

"How can you be so sure, musician?" Natoki asked.

"Come on, guys," Thibodeau said. "They fell for the Obliteration Option, didn't they?"

Several snickers followed that and Thibodeau tapped Max on the shoulder as he moved toward the exit. "Come on, Max."

"Where to, Tobias?" Ghun'jur asked.

"Back to the Recreation Center," Thibodeau said. "As I recall we were right in the middle of a set when this ridiculous situation began to manifest itself. Now that it's over, I plan on finishing the concert."

"Are you serious?" Blanton asked and rose from the command chair.

"Absolutely," Thibodeau responded. "This ship has some traumatized passengers who need to have their souls soothed by some good old fashioned melodies right about now. I think that our Soviet friends learned a valuable lesson today: only fools rush in before knowing what they are getting themselves into. That, my friends, reminds me of a song sung just a couple of centuries ago by a man the people of the Earth often referred to as The King. I plan on going back down to the Recreation Center, assembling my band, and adding that song to my set beginning today. You're all welcome to come down and listen for a while. In fact, I recommend it."

Tobias Thibodeau, a man most people across the Known Grid-Levels of Space referred to simply as The Player, raised his hand in salute toward the prone body of Captain Karl Adelson, turned on his heels and disappeared through the entrance doors of the Donello's bridge.

Several minutes later, a com-link hooked up to the Recreation Center was letting the softest of melodies and a voice of pure magic flow unhindered into the small confines of the Donello's bridge. Tobias Thibodeau's rich voice sounded very much like a man once referred to as The King as he sang to thousands of people in the large room several decks below.

"Wise men say, only fools rush in..." Doug Blanton heard and couldn't help but smile as he checked the coordinates on his console for Martensburgengrad.

Caught In A Trap

The smooth tones sang loud in his ears, and Maximillian Gun'jhur let his head sway with the music. The auditorium was enormous, one of the largest rooms under one roof that Max had ever seen but the acoustics were wonderful and the many thousands in the crowd seemed to be very happy.

This song was a slower one, a piece that Max had heard his band play many times in the past. Every square inch of the broad dance floor was seemingly covered with dancing couples and, from what he could see, most of them were looking deep into each other's eyes, holding each other closely and enjoying the opportunity to move a bit slower than they had been through the previous set.

Just a few minutes ago, Toby had launched into an entire series of ancient Rock & Roll songs, most dating back to more than a century earlier, and the crowd was eating it up. Max deeply enjoyed all of the older melodies, the music so sweet and smooth, but the velvet voice of the man singing lead seemed to be holding everyone in a trance. Max wasn't surprised, though. No, not in the least. Tobias Thibodeau often worked this kind of magic on a crowd. Max had seen it with his own eyes many times…and it never ceased to amaze him.

Toby was currently mixing it up with songs about everything from hound dogs to jailhouses, Teddy Bears to some kind of crazy blue shoes. *Where does he get this stuff,* Max thought and laughed. *Blue shoes? Only this man could hold sway over thousands of people with a song about blue shoes.*

Max glanced one more time over the many dancing couples and smiled. Toby was in his element here. The four other members of the band were as well. It never failed to dawn on Max that these musicians just played so much better when in the tall man's company. He'd heard them all play individually or with other groups but they never sounded quite as good as they did when Toby was singing on stage.

The song wound down and the crowd sensed it. Almost as one massive being, they stopped dancing, faced the stage and broke into a raucous round of applause. Toby, modest as ever, took two bows, motioned to his band mates as if they deserved all the credit and then slowly made his way off stage. That last set had been Toby's third attempt to end the show for the night and, if Max knew his star attraction at all, three encores were as far as Toby would go.

They had been playing this gig as Tall -T and The Wayfarers, a smaller band known in this region of Grid-Space for their wonderful covers of the older rock classics. By the sound of the applause still filling the enormous room even now, several minutes after the band had left the stage, Max knew his musicians had won more than their fair share of additional fans tonight.

Max watched as a young couple approached the bar and took two seats not far from his position. The girl was very pretty, about five feet tall, and her boyfriend looked to be an athletic type. They were both smiling and still clapping with the others as Max leaned over and said, "Those guys were really something, eh?"

"Amazing," the young man said and his pretty date agreed. "They sounded just like this guy I was listening to over the Grid a few months ago who blew me away," the youngster continued. "They called the guy The Player and I've been trying to find everything he's recorded ever since."

"Ever find any?" Max asked, now very interested.

"Oh, yeah, I've found dozens," the kid said and smiled.

"We play them non-stop," the girl said, her voice sounding distant, like she was still in some far off dream-place. "Those guys up there tonight sounded just like them. I mean, like they were the same band. You know what I mean?"

Max smiled and nodded several times very slowly. "Yes, I do," he said and looked back over the crowd. "I most certainly do."

*   *   *

"Max!" a muffled voice called from the other side of his cabin's door and he rustled in the small bed. "Max, come on, it's time to go!"

Max rolled over on to his back and tried to focus his eyes on the small clock near the bed. "Christ," he swore at the time and kicked his feet over the edge. "Why so early?"

The small door opened, letting in a very bright light from the corridor and Tobias Thibodeau stuck his head inside. "Because it's time to go."

"Alright, Tobias, alright," Max said and stood up on shaky legs. "Give me a second."

"Just one and make it fast," the tall musician said and let the door close behind him. Max gathered up his few belongings, dressed quickly and washed his face in the sink of the small bathroom that came with his room. Moments later he stepped into the corridor, his one small travel bag strapped across his back, and squinted at the bright light shining in through the massive view windows.

No matter how many times he came back to the Moon, he would never get used to seeing the landscape looking so much like Earth's. Although an atmosphere had been installed around the Moon by Becker Industrial Associates more than twenty-five years ago, Max would never stop thinking of the small white satellite image he had seen in his textbooks while growing up in school. It just didn't seem right to have grass and trees and open air on the small spheroid that circled the Earth. But Becker was paying for this gig and he wasn't going to pass up such a grand opportunity for his band to entertain the masses during the organization's 50th Anniversary Extravaganza.

Taking a deep breath of some of the cleanest air he'd tasted in quite some time, Max turned and found the other members in his party standing together underneath a tree in the small square outside the Becker HQ Building about thirty meters away.

"It's about time you woke up," Dimitri Godansky said and laughed at the disheveled appearance of the band's manager as Max approached. "We're almost late for our appointment on Earth with Fantasticon Productions."

"Give me a break," Max said to the band's Lead Guitarist. "That meet isn't for at least another six hours."

"Yeah, well, breakfast wouldn't have hurt too badly, either," Martino Velez said, his fingers twirling a set of drumsticks around in an elaborate pattern effortlessly.

"You're always hungry, Tino," Rider Boone said as he messed with the volume controls on his bass guitar and gently plucked at the strings. With its self-contained power pack, the instrument required no outside energy source. In fact, none of the instruments that this band was using required outside power. The miracle of micro-nucleonics at work.

"I could have used some food this morning, too," Swayne Morrison said. Max knew the thin keyboardist tried never to miss a breakfast.

"Anyway, we're not done here yet," Toby said and motioned toward a white-haired older gentleman who had just exited the main doors to Becker's elaborate home base. Max turned and immediately recognized Hans Becker, the CEO of the organization himself, and the man's assistant as the two men approached the band.

Toby quickly extended his hand toward the grinning man and bade him good morning. "Thank you so much, Mr. Thibodeau, for your wonderful performance last night," Becker said and nodded in acknowledgement to the other members of the band. "Mr. Gun'jhur, my compliments to your people here. They put on quite a show, quite a show indeed."

"They'll be talking about this for the next five e-years in the Upper-Levels," the young assistant said nervously but quieted at a glare from Becker.

"And Mr. Cho," Becker said to the mid-sized Asian man who hadn't yet uttered a word since Max joined the group. "Brilliant effects during the entire performance, young man. I was deeply impressed with your fine touch and nuances around the pyrotechnic displays."

"Thank you, sir," Ti Cho said and nodded once from his position sitting atop the stone embankment surrounding the tree.

"Gentlemen, it is to my great sorrow that I have to see you leave so soon," Becker said. "I wish you could stay and enjoy the day in browsing through our on-site museum and historical tour."

"Thank you very kindly, Mr. Becker, sir," Max said and glanced down at his watch. "We would love to take you up on your hospitality, but we have an urgent meeting on Earth in just a bit and we have to be moving on."

"Understood, fine sirs, understood," Becker said and clapped his hands together. "With the amount of sheer talent I was witness to last night, it isn't any wonder to me that your time is precious and your schedules full. Shall I make payment now?"

"Yes, sir, that would be grand," Max said and began to look through his bag for his Mini-Financial Manager. The gadget was no larger than his palm and acted as the band's own private bank. It collected fees, transferred funds, made payments, deposited various monies into dozens of InterGridactic Accounts and even allowed him to perform many different types of investment transactions on several dozen other planets. A very tidy and convenient bit of mechanics but not worth a damn thing if Max couldn't find it.

"I'm so sorry, Mr. Becker," Max stumbled a bit. "I seem to have left my MFM in the shuttle, sir. I'll only be a minute, please excuse me."

"Nonsense," Becker said and began to walk toward the mini starport his organization had built on the Moon many years ago. "I have just been told that a representative of my fiercest competitor, Calabrio Design & Manufacturing, is due to land here at any moment in order to discuss urgent business, whatever his notion of that might be, so I'll walk with you in order to meet the scoundrel at my very own gates."

"That would be our pleasure, sir," Toby said and began to make strong headway with his long strides.

As The Player himself and the head of Becker Industrial Associates made small talk, Max excused himself quietly from the conversation and began to walk ahead, eager to find the small machine. With so much of vital importance stored within his MFM's memory chips, he would feel completely and utterly vulnerable until the very moment that he was, once again, holding the thing in his hands.

Their shuttle was still sitting on the small pad, closest to the starport's main gate, and Max could see another larger shuttle, looking somewhat like a medium-sized troop transport, heading for the pad directly adjacent to it. He shielded his eyes momentarily from the blast of downdraft as the sleek vessel met the tarmac on a gentle cushion of air and entered the pass code on their rented Valkyrie—326.

He entered the main corridor of their small shuttle and headed immediately for the cockpit, where he had been flying the thing a day earlier. His piloting skills had saved the band some serious money in piloting fees over the past few years. Of course, he left the long-hauls to commercial or private transport companies but, short hops like the one from Jupiter's LookOut Station to the Moon and Earth, he piloted with ease.

Max sighed with relief as he saw the tiny machine lying on the dashboard in the cockpit. *How on Earth did I ever leave the thing out of my sight?* he wondered and hurriedly made his way forward to grab up the tiny device. Max barely heard the screams and brief spat of charger fire that came from the next landing pad over as he maneuvered through the rented shuttle's interior.

*   *   *

"Here he is now," Hans Becker said as the extraction doors to the larger shuttle that had just landed hissed open not twenty meters away. "Please excuse me for a moment, Toby, as I greet Justin Calabrio and his party."

"Absolutely, Mr. Becker," Toby said and turned to look into the wide-open doors of the Valkyrie, wondering where Max had gotten himself off to. Glancing quickly back over his shoulder, he found it a mystery why anyone would need to bring a vessel that large to the Moon for something as simple as a business meeting. *The filthy rich,* he smirked and peered once again into the dark interior of the Valkyrie, *I'll never understand them...*

He heard the sounds of many boots hitting the tarmac, sounds that were quite unfamiliar coming from a supposed privately chartered vessel, and turned back toward the newly arrived shuttle with concern. Hans Becker's eyes were wide open in disbelief as a small cadre of very heavily armed men in military style fatigues exited the shuttle and pointed their weapons in his direction.

"What in the hell is going on here, Toby?" Dimitri asked as at least twenty pseudo-military men fanned out to point weapons at everyone in the general vicinity.

"I don't have any idea, Dimitri," Toby said. "But just stay alert here and no sudden moves."

"As you say, boss," Rider Boone said and let his guitar drop lightly to the ground. Three men in dark clothing, helmets with visors down and some big black guns, surrounded the small party of musicians and motioned for them to head back toward the Becker HQ Building.

"I don't know about you, Max," Toby said in a slightly raised voice. "But I think I'm going to be sick. Yep, that's definitely the word, Max, sick, sick sick…"

Maximillian Gun'jhur heard the words of his prime talent and nodded to himself in understanding from his hidden position within the smaller Valkyrie. Some type of Corporate Coup was taking place just outside of the thin composite walls of his shuttlecraft and, by the looks of the big bulky weapons being held by their new visitors, this was not going to be a pleasant day. Toby's message had been clear, however, one of them was going to be getting "sick" soon and it would have to be his job to make the situation well again.

* * *

"Just what in the name of God is going on here, Justin," Hans Becker said as the Junior Vice President of his strongest competitor walked down the ramp of the large Iroquois Class shuttlecraft. "How dare you bring men with guns here, to my base of operations. I demand an explanation!"

"Shut up old man," Justin Calabrio spat and motioned for the tallest man among the soldiers to do the quieting. The butt of the big man's charger rammed sharply into Becker's lower abdomen and the older man clutched his ribs and hit the tarmac hard.

"Hey!" Tom Bellins, Hans Becker's personal assistant, exclaimed and stepped forward to stop the man's next assault with the rifle's butt. With a speed possessed of only the better-trained mercenaries, the soldier stepped back, righted his charger and fired point blank into the young man's face. What was left of Bellins' head slapped wetly to the tarmac while the remainder of his corpse twitched uncontrollably on the way down.

Calabrio's eyes grew wide and he fixed his glare on the tall man behind the blackened helmet visor. His fury was evident but there was nothing he could do now. The first step toward making this hostile takeover of Becker Industrial Associates official had just been taken. Now he would have to come up with a valid reason that would stand against the sternest of inquiries by the Universal Corporate Council as to why a man had been killed during the initial meeting between the two parties.

"Now you know just how serious I am, Hans," Calabrio said. As a Vice President of Calabrio Design and Manufacturing, the first corporation to go back to Mars after the suicide bombing of the first U.E.N. colony on the red planet took place in 2061, he was extremely proud to be the man who would lead his father's organization to its first major expansion in more than a generation. Becker, with their luxury installation on the Moon and the breathable atmosphere that they had succeeded in pumping around it in 2089, had always been the one major obstacle to Calabrio's growth throughout the U.E.N. Now, today, that would end. Right here, with this boldest of moves, Justin Calabrio would put an end to Becker's reign over the realm of InterGridactic industrial manufacturing for once and for all. "Today marks a new day for our two organizations, Hans. My father wishes he could be here but he has more important things to tend to. Like informing our mutual colleagues, suppliers, investors and customers of our upcoming merger."

"That will never happen, you punk," Becker said from his place on the ground and spit at Calabrio's feet.

Justin stopped breathing momentarily as anger built up red and hot within him but he worked to control himself. He needed some semblance of self-control now more than ever. If this meeting were to result in the death of Hans Becker, he and his father would never obtain the backing they would need from both the Universal Corporate Council and the local sector of the U.E.N. Mergers Committee in order to make this takeover work.

He willed himself to be still and saw the large form of mercenary leader, Mick Sawyer, step forward once again with the butt of his charger.

"No," Calabrio growled and Sawyer stopped his right arm's forward momentum. "I will handle this for now with diplomacy and tact. They have seen that we have no qualms about hurting them physically by the foolish actions of that now headless man on the ground," Calabrio said, indicating the body of Tom Bellins lying not too far away. "Now we will do this thing quickly and peacefully. Or, things will turn nasty. Do you hear me, Hans? You wouldn't want your stubborn ways to result in more deaths, now would you?"

The older man lifted himself somewhat shakily to his feet and stood to face Calabrio. "Your father most likely knows nothing about this, Justin," Becker said. "He is a fine and decent man, a man who it has been my pleasure to do business with over these past few decades. He is not a man who would hire thugs with guns and send his son here to kill and intimidate. No, Justin, these are your actions. And now, those actions carry blood with them. Blood that is on your hands, you pathetic waste."

Justin Calabrio lost his grip momentarily and swung a vicious open right hand against Hans Becker's face. The old man staggered but didn't go down, a small trickle of blood flowed steadily from his busted lip. "We will do this now, old man!"

"Or what? You will have these men kill more of my employees?" Becker shouted.

"Yes, and that will be blood on your hands," Calabrio said. "As much blood as it takes!"

* * *

"We are just a band of musicians," Toby said for the fourth time in as many minutes. "Mr. Becker was on his way to meet with your…party…and decided to walk with us to our rented shuttle. We had played at the 50th Anniversary Party last night, that's all."

"You can keep talking," the man behind the visor said. "I don't care who you are or where you were going, but no one leaves here until this business is done."

"How long will that be?" Dimitri Godansky asked and the merc looked up sharply at his distinctly Soviet accent.

"Are you one of them lousy Russians?" the soldier asked, half-raising his weapon and taking a step forward.

"He is one of my band members," Toby said and stepped in between the advancing soldier and his lead guitar player. "That is all. We are musicians, we will cause no harm by leaving here. We are not concerned with this business, do you understand?"

The man tried to look around the tall form of Tobias Thibodeau one more time to where Dimitri stood but settled back to look up into Toby's eyes. "I'll say it again, I don't care who you are, you guys aren't going anywhere."

"How about his medicine?" Rider Boone asked, indicating their tall lead singer.

"I don't care..." the mercenary began.

"The man needs his medicine and it's on that shuttle of ours," Boone interrupted the soldier and pointed out the window of the small office they were in to where the shuttle still sat parked on the tarmac in the mini-starport, not too very far away.

"What's his condition?"

"Heart problems," Boone began but Toby twirled around to fix him with an angry glare.

"Shut up, Boone!" Thibodeau exclaimed. "Don't be bringing that up now!"

"If you don't get that medicine you could die, Toby, I'm just looking out for you!"

"Don't do me any favors," Toby growled but Swayne Morrison stepped forward.

"Look, our leader here needs his meds," Morrison said to the merc. "But he's too proud to ask you for them so I'm telling you myself, he will die if he doesn't get his meds and get them quick."

"I said shut up about that, Swayne!" Toby yelled.

"So, why don't you go tell your head goon out there about this situation and maybe we can stop something from getting ugly in here."

"Let me check on this," the mercenary stammered and opened the door a crack. He called for another man in fatigues and helmet with visor in place and whispered to him for a few seconds before the door to the small office they had been thrown into closed again.

"I don't want any special attention," Toby said and seemed to stagger for a minute. "I don't want…want…anything…"

"What's the matter, Toby?" Rider asked as Thibodeau crashed against a nearby wall and slid to the ground.

The room exploded into action then as the band members rushed to their fallen leader and the man with the gun hopped from one foot to the other, trying to figure out what in the hell to do. Boone and Morrison were both yelling at him to do something and Ti Cho had ripped open Toby's shirt to start checking his heart beat.

"It's erratic!" Cho screamed, his high voice echoing off the walls in the enclosed space. "He's going to die!"

"Jesus, bring him to the Infirmary in this building!" the soldier shouted.

"His meds are in the shuttle!" Godansky yelled.

"No! No shuttle! Bring him to the Infirmary," the soldier yelled. "In this building, not outside!"

"Christ, he's dying!" Boone said and bent to lift the motionless Toby to his feet.

The mercenary opened the door to the office and motioned for another of his men to come over and help the struggling band of musicians as they filed out of the door and into the corridor. "Take them to the Infirmary, this man is dying!"

"Where in the hell is that?" the new mercenary asked.

"Shit if I know, Porter," the other soldier said. "Just find the damn place and get him to it. If we let one of them die over something as stupid as this, Calabrio is going to have another frigging fit."

"Crap, let's go," Porter yelled and, at gunpoint, the band members rambled down the corridor, trying to support the large lanky frame of Tobias Thibodeau between them. The original guard slumped up against a wall and tried to calm his breathing and racing heart. *What a frigging circus this had turned out to be*, he thought to himself and looked down both ends of the long hallway to make sure that no one else had seen or heard the ordeal that had just taken place.

* * *

"Listen, Justin…I'm not going to just hand over my corporation to you and your father…do you understand?" Becker said through bleeding lips, his right eye bruised shut from the beating he had already suffered.

"Don't make this so hard on yourself, Hans," Calabrio urged, the panic in his voice rising as he realized that the situation was spiraling totally out of control. The old man was not cooperating, one man was already dead and this was not going at all as he had planned. Becker had been right about one thing, though, his father didn't know anything about this operation. Justin was acting on his own. Acting toward more than tripling the size of Calabrio Design & Manufacturing in one swift and decisive move.

A move that would place him on the top rung of his father's corporate ladder. A position now occupied by Justin's older brother, Miguel. *This has to work*, the young Calabrio thought, *and it has to work soon. This is taking much too long…*

Sawyer reared back and struck Hans Becker once again across the mouth. More blood splattered against the walls of the CEO's plush office and on to the Transfer of Ownership documents strewn atop his ornate desk. All of this could have been done electronically, using old man Becker's thumbprint on an extraction screen as a seal of approval on the deal, but deep down Justin knew…his father would not accept anything short of Becker's true signature on the actual paperwork once the details of the merger were presented to him back on Corpura.

The chair that Becker was tied to fell to the floor as Sawyer's blow struck home and the old man let out a long groan of pain. Sawyer lifted him back into a sitting position with ease and pulled his right fist back yet again…

* * *

The doors to the Infirmary opened and the lone doctor whirled around in surprise. "What is going on here?" he demanded but the musicians just brushed past him and laid the still unmoving body of Tobias Thibodeau on the single examining table in the center of the white room.

"Treat this man, doctor, he's dying" the soldier with the gun said as he leaned over the backs of one of the musicians, trying for a better look at the dying man on the table.

Max Gun'jhur reached a hand into the white medical smock he was wearing and extracted a syringe that the real head doctor of Becker Industrial Associates, a man now hiding in the small office behind the examination room, had told him would knock out a three-hundred pound man. He found a good spot on the man's exposed neck, underneath the helmet but just above the man's shirt, and plunged the needle in deeply. The man jerked around and grabbed for Max but Rider Boone had been waiting and he crashed into the soldier, forcing him to the ground. The man tried to fight back at first but quickly stopped moving once the drug took effect.

All of the men stopped moving for a moment to collect their breaths. "Nice to see you, Max," Toby said and winked. "Any trouble getting here?"

"It's a long story, Tobias, I'll tell you some other time" Max said, walked over to the small door separating the office from the Infirmary proper and opened it up. "Thanks, Doc," he said and a small man with gray hair popped his head into the opening.

"That little mixture should work to keep that man unconscious for about five or six hours," the doctor said and watched as Toby climbed off the white table in the middle of the room. "What are your plans?"

"Can't really tell you right now, Doc," Toby said and fixed Ti Cho with a crooked smile. "You just had to rip open the shirt, didn't you?"

"It seemed like the right thing to do at the time, boss," Cho said and leaned down to pick up the mercenary's fallen weapon.

Rider Boone and Dimitri Godansky lifted the merc up on to the table and began removing the man's uniform and helmet. The young face that was exposed couldn't have been any older than eighteen or nineteen. *Certainly not yet over twenty*, Max thought in disapproval and plucked the blaster from the man's hip holster to hand it over to Swayne Morrison.

"So, now what?" Max asked and looked at Toby for guidance. The other members of the band followed suit and Max smiled. *Even in times of turmoil, he's ever our leader...*

"Well, one thing's for sure, those guns won't do us any good," Toby said. "We're musicians and engineers, not soldiers."

"It feels good to have one, though," Rider said and Max found himself having to agree.

"We need to figure out how to turn the tables on this situation," Toby said.

"If only we'd have been just a few minutes earlier in leaving this place," Martino Velez said, his eyes glaring at Max.

"Don't blame Max on this one," Toby said and leaned against the table. "Whatever this is, we're caught up in it and that's not going to change. We somehow got caught in a trap here and we have to find our way out."

"What can we do?" Dimitri asked and silence ruled the small infirmary for several minutes.

"What is this all about?" Toby asked then and started pacing about the room. "I mean, what is this really all about?"

"Let's see, it's a very hostile takeover for one," Max offered.

"One of the most hostile I've ever seen," Rider joked but nobody laughed.

"And what's the underlying force behind such a move on the part of Calabrio?" Toby asked and let the question linger for several moments.

Max felt the weight of his MFM then in the side pocket of his cargo-style pants and realized what this was really all about. He pulled out the small machine and turned it on. "Money," he said.

All eyes turned to him and the Mini-Financial Manager he was holding in his right hand. "Bingo," Toby said.

*　*　*

"This isn't working, Mr. Calabrio," Mick Sawyer said in a very low tone to Justin about twelve feet away from where Becker sat bleeding and semi-conscious. "This man is not about to do what you want him to do. Not voluntarily or under threat of physical violence to his person."

"Just make him do it, do you understand?" Calabrio growled. "And do it fast!"

Sawyer stiffened at the younger man's demeaning tone and steeled himself from lashing out at the man who was paying him for this job. "Listen, Calabrio," Sawyer said through gritted teeth. "I don't have any jurisdiction on this little rock, neither do you. Although, if we get this old son of a bitch to sign off on the paperwork then, technically, nothing we have done here will have been illegal…if we don't do it soon and the local police show up before the Articles of your little merger have been accepted…they will have the right to arrest all of us and charge us with murder."

"Screw that, Sawyer," Calabrio said and glanced across the room at the groaning form of Becker, still tied to his chair. "I hired your people because I was told you were the best in the business. At least, locally. Now show me some of that talent and get this job done!"

Sawyer took a deep breath and glanced at the bleeding old man too. Sure, he was a soldier, but beating up defenseless old men in their places of business was not what he considered an honorable job. "In order to finish this thing we're going to need to use a little bit of external pressure."

"Haven't you been exerting just a little bit of external pressure on him already?" Calabrio shot back.

"I don't mean on the old man, Calabrio," Sawyer said. "I mean on someone close to him. Someone maybe like his secretary, a trusted female employee."

"Why female?" Calabrio asked, the concern very evident on his face.

"Because it will serve to make him bend more quickly to our will," Sawyer said from behind his visor. "Believe me, we shouldn't have to do more than threaten to hurt the girl, whoever it is we pick. But it has to be someone he works with on a daily basis, someone he will feel somewhat attached to."

Calabrio took the several seconds of silence to think this through and try to convince himself of the validity of this new tactic. Sawyer saw the mixture of emotions play across the younger man's features and noticed the time slowly ticking away… making this situation more hopeless with each passing second.

"Alright!" Calabrio shouted. "Alright! Find your woman and find her quick. This needs to be taken care of quickly!"

* * *

Ti Cho worked his way through the subterranean access tunnel that led from Becker's HQ Building directly to the mini-starport located next door. Rider Boone had hacked into the building's corporate records and brought up a set of schematics on the Infirmary's lone workstation.

They had learned that, not only had this building been built with the underground access way in order to conceal the comings and goings of the major corporate players who passed through this place on a daily basis, but that there were separate tunnels leading to each of the individual landing pads as well.

His effects equipment for the show last night were stowed safely aboard the shuttle, in one of the lower cargo compartments built into the Valkyrie's fuselage. The small amount of pyrotechnics that he hadn't used during the 50th Anniversary Extravaganza the night before should be just enough to cause the diversion that was the key to Toby's plan.

He checked his printout of the underground labyrinth of tunnels and chose the one that should lead directly to the small landing pad on which sat their rented shuttle. After several minutes of navigating the long and narrow side-tunnel, he came to the end and found metal rungs sticking out of the concrete. Ti looked up and saw that there weren't any more than maybe twenty-five or thirty rungs. He climbed the metal ladder up the short distance to the landing pad itself and slowly slipped back the latch to the access door that led to the surface.

The heavily used hatch lifted open easily, without a hint of a squeak on well lubricated hinges, and Ti took a nervous glance around. He grinned at the total absence of guards around the landing pads. He could see one or two men with guns at the small entrance to the starport itself, but no one was currently located in or around the many vessels situated on several of the pads within the complex. It was bright out there, though, as it always was on this side of the Moon facing the Earth, bright enough for him to be seen unless he was very careful. The Becker HQ Building was not very far away and there could be many sets of eyes peering through windows in an effort to find someone like himself skulking around the starport. Ti knew that he had to do this and do it fast. If he thought about it anymore, he would only freak himself out. Taking in a deep breath, Ti brought up his resolve and swung the hatch open.

* * *

"Ok, I'm into Calabrio's system," Rider Boone said from his seat in front of the Infirmary's small workstation. "I have access to everything but I need to make this quick. No doubt the Calabrio's computer-tech staff has safeguards and alarm systems in place to shut down any attempts like this to pirate their electronic records."

"Let me in there," Swayne Morrison said and took Rider's place in front of the computer. "Get me into their financial records, Rider, I'll only need a few minutes."

"Try to make that less than a minute and we'll consider ourselves lucky," Rider said as his fingers flew fast over the keyboard from Swayne's right side. "Ok, you're in but make it quick, I could see the first phase of a firewall system taking action as I was bypassing their coding structure."

"No problem, guys," Morrison said with a grin as his fingers replaced those of Boone's. The musicians looked on in wonder as their keyboardist played havoc with Calabrio's financial records. "Let me show you what a former accountant with the Universal Corporate Council can do to royally screw any organization that used to cause them grief."

"Isn't this a little bit illegal?" Max asked, his eyes transfixed in awe at the sheer speculation of what all the numbers flashing across the tiny screen might mean.

"Not in the least bit…well, ok, maybe a little," Morrison began. "But look at it this way, these guys are performing a hostile takeover of the worst sort right now. Their actions only become legal once Becker signs off on their Merger documents. If that doesn't happen before the local law enforcement catches wind of what is happening here and decide to interfere, then the Calabrio people will be guilty of killing that young assistant of Becker's and of assault on Becker himself."

"Strange how Corporate Law works out there in the Grids," Toby said and shook his head in disgust. "If Becker signs, then that young man's murder becomes a small hurdle that will be easily overcome in the Merger Committee Hearings. That's why I stick with music, to get away from all the crap that takes place in the corporate world."

"And a very wise decision that is, Tobias," Max said with a grin, patting the tall man on the back. "For you and me both."

Toby smirked at that and turned his attention back to the small flat screen where Morrison's fingers were still flying, replaced every few seconds by Boone's as another obstacle forced into their electronic pathway by Calabrio's tech people needed to be bypassed. So many numbers were flashing across the screen, InterGridactic dollars by the billions, disappearing from one side and appearing on the other. Suddenly the numbers were replaced by the wording in corporate legalize of a very official looking document.

"Max, let's have your MFM," Morrison said and held out his hand impatiently. Gun'jhur handed the small device over and Morrison quickly connected to the terminal he was working on. More documents flew across the screen, including the agreement made by Becker with Tall - T And The Wayfarers the night before, just before the celebration began. Becker's thumbprint had sealed that deal and had been stored in the MFM's memory. Morrison used that thumbprint now to seal the deal on the Legal and Financial Documents that he had just drawn up. The senior Calabrio's thumbprint had also been used from a document stored in their legal records a few seconds ago. Now with the legal approvals of both Corporation's CEO's on the new documentation, the plan that Toby had come up with could enter the final stage.

"That's it, I'm done," Morrison said and quickly vacated the seat so that Boone could get back to work, hiding their electronic trails and creating blockades and decoys that hopefully could not be traced back to this medical terminal within the Becker HQ.

"Done," Boone announced and stood up to face his friends. "Thank you, Doctor, for allowing us to utilize your workstation."

"If this little plan of yours works out, gentlemen, it is I who'll be thanking you, of that there is no doubt," the short older man said. Toby shook hands with the man and motioned to the still unconscious soldier on the table.

"If he wakes up early, Doc, feel free to use a blunt object to render him asleep again," Toby offered. "I'm sure he deserves it."

"Don't you worry my tall friend," the doctor laughed. "I have my ways, he will not pose a threat to anyone for the next several hours at least."

"That's good to know," Thibodeau said and addressed his colleagues. "Ok, let's find that hidden accessway to the Upper-Levels of this place and take care of business."

"Amen to that," Max said, adjusting the uncomfortable soldier's uniform he was wearing. The small communications device embedded in the helmet had been disconnected shortly after they had gotten the uniform off the motionless merc. All of them knew that another of the soldiers could be coming to the Infirmary to check on their comrade in arms at any moment. "The sooner we can clean this mess up, the better."

* * *

One of Sawyer's men dragged the young woman into Becker's office and forced her roughly into one of the chairs facing the old man. Sawyer cracked open a small vile of smelling salts and waved it under Becker's nose. The man stirred and opened his eyes to take in the scene around him.

Justin Calabrio and the large head of the mercenary group was standing on either side of Melanie Crawford, his personal secretary, as she sat in one of the chairs that was positioned on the other side of his desk. He had been wheeled around the desk in his chair and she now faced him, the large soldier's hands positioned on her narrow shoulders, holding her down. Becker felt the anger rise up inside him as he saw the bruise on her left cheek and the small trickle of dried blood that ran from a bloody scab on that same corner of her mouth.

"You bastards!" He growled and strained hard against his bonds.

"Now, now, Hans," Justin Calabrio said and ran his fingers along Melanie's jaw line. "Don't upset the young lady, here."

"You would do this thing, Justin?" Becker asked and fixed the young man with an angry glare.

"Sign the paperwork, Hans," Calabrio said in a low and even tone. "And we won't even have to think about that option."

"You son of a bitch…" Becker said and leaned his head back to stare at the ceiling of his office. He slowly brought his head back down to look into the terrified and crying eyes of Melanie Crawford. "Forgive me, Melanie, I never thought that they would stoop so low."

"Mr. Calabrio…" Crawford began in a shaky voice but Sawyer smacked her harshly across the face. The girl screamed and fell out of her chair to land roughly on the carpet. Sawyer leaned down and grabbed her by the arm, lifting her and throwing her into the chair once again in one quick and seamless movement.

"Be quiet!" He barked and the girl sat there sobbing.

Hans Becker watched this in astonishment and felt all the fight go out of him. He looked at Melanie, new blood dripping from her mouth, and felt tears of shame and helplessness flow down his face. "You are both monsters…" he muttered.

"Will you sign now, Hans?" Calabrio asked and rolled Becker's chair closer to the desk where the blood-spattered legal documents sat, awaiting his signature.

"Yes, yes, I'll sign anything you want me to," Becker said through gritted teeth. "Just don't hurt her anymore you animals."

Justin felt a massive release in his chest then and took in a deep breath. He felt as if he hadn't breathed in at least a year but this all looked as if it would finally come to fruition. "Release his arms and hand him the pen," he said to Sawyer who was already at work loosening the old man's bonds. "Are you sure that you have the right chemicals to erase that blood from the paperwork?"

"We've done this sort of thing before, Calabrio," Sawyer said as Becker's hands became free.

Becker leaned forward over the documents that would legally sign the ownership of his corporation over to this young little fool and glanced once more at Melanie's terrified face. "Don't worry, Mel," Becker said. "This goes no further."

Reaching forward he touched pen to paper and hesitated for a fraction of an instant. All of his years of hard work, all of his hopes and dreams for his organization…all of it coming down to this.

He sighed once and began to draw the pen down to start the "H" in his signature. His hand got no further as the large Iroquois Class shuttle that had transported Calabrio and his band of goons to the Moon blew up in the starport adjacent to the Becker HQ Building. The huge explosion shattered windows throughout the sprawling complex and everyone inside Becker's office hit the floor.

* * *

Max and the musicians had been climbing up the cold concrete stairs in the secure-access area of the Becker HQ Building when the first explosion shook the enormous structure. Everyone reached out for handrails and walls to steady themselves as the building vibrated. The sound of shattering glass was loud enough to be heard through the sound-proofed coating of the stairwell's walls and several loud thumps sounded from outside as large pieces of debris bounced off the structure's exterior.

That's one, Max thought and glanced back to see that the rest of his friends were all still behind him on the stairs. The visor of his helmet was up so that he could see within the darkened confines of this secret exit to and from the Upper-Levels of the corporate stronghold. Soon, in a matter of minutes, he would lower the thing and burst through the hidden door into Becker's office, where Toby had assumed the business at hand would be taking place.

While the group marched toward the hidden hatchway that led to this area of the building from the Infirmary, Max had held them at gunpoint, acting as if he were one of the merc's. Since he was the only one that hadn't been seen by any of the invading soldiers and could not be recognized, he had to be the one to don the uniform and play the bad-guy. So far, he had been lucky, no one had stopped to engage them in small talk. They had seen several large meeting rooms and other open spaces filled with Becker employees being guarded mostly by just a single man.

The group had agreed that the mercenary forces had to be spread pretty thin in order to be covering all of the Becker personnel within the complex. This worked very much in their favor, as all of the armed men were much too busy to be worried about where one of their colleagues was leading the small band of musicians.

They had entered the hatchway very quickly, the small door had been located quite close to the Security Entrance and, as they had passed by, more than a few angry guards could be seen sitting on the floor of the mid-sized office with their arms tied back.

We could use a few more weapons, Max thought as he realized that, aside from the half-charger he was holding, the only other weapon the group possessed was the small blaster taken off the merc back in the Infirmary. That gun now sat pressed against the back of Dimitri Godansky, fit snugly between his skin and the waistband of his tight slacks. The dull black butt of the pistol was being covered by the untucked portion of his long shirt. Dimitri had been a member of the Soviet military prior to the signing of the Grid-Division Treaty of 2100 and, although he was the best suited among them to masquerade as one of the mercenaries, his absence from the small group of musicians could arouse some suspicion. So, Max had been given "Guard" duty and the band of men had tried their best to traverse the first floor corridors without raising any attention.

Now, they found themselves just on the other side of the door to Becker's office and the entire group could feel the tension hanging thick in the processed oxygen of the stairwell.

"Are we ready, gentlemen?" Toby asked and the others nodded. "Ok, remember now, let's play this smart and not go trigger happy. We don't want to have to shoot anyone although, if they start bringing weapons to bear, I want you two to start firing," he said, motioning to Max and Dimitri.

"Understood," Godansky answered and Max simply gulped once and nodded.

"Alright, now Ti should be giving us our GO signal at any moment. Once we hear that, it's through the door…understood?"

"Sure thing, boss," Rider Boone said, the anxiety on his face fully evident in the dull glow of the dim lamps spread evenly throughout the stairwell. Martino Velez leaned gently toward the door and put an ear to the cold metal surface. After several seconds, he faced the group and shook his head. "I can't hear a thing, I have no clue if there's anyone in there or not."

"Oh, they're in there," Toby said and readied himself for action. "You can bet, if that Calabrio kid took Hans Becker anywhere, it was right to this place. He wouldn't have something like this happen anywhere else but right here in the old man's office."

"I hope you're right, Toby," Max said and gripped the stock of his charger a little tighter.

"Don't you worry, Max," Tobias Thibodeau said. "Don't you worry."

Just then a second explosion sounded outside, this one smaller, and Max winced at the fact that their rental had to be sacrificed. *At least the insurance that he had taken at the dealership would cover the loss of the vessel…although, some of their equipment would be harder to replace…*

"That's our GO!" Toby said and Max wrenched down on the door's access bar. He rushed through and began screaming, just as they had planned it.

* * *

Sawyer had hit the deck again as another small shuttle on the tarmac of the starport exploded, a rush of heat actually making it into Becker's office through the blown-out windows, and he swore. This mission had gone to shit and he wanted it to be over already.

Just then, a part of the wall across the office crashed open and one of his men, with visor down, stumbled in screaming, "They're attacking us! They're attacking us!"

Everyone froze for an instant, including Sawyer, as he didn't want to fire on one of his own men amidst the confusion of the situation. The man continued his headlong rush into the office, weapon pointed downward, and crashed into Becker, driving him to the floor. As he had passed, the man had managed to reach out and grab for the girl, too, knocking her down as well.

Other men were running into the office now, too many for his mind to identify as friend or foe, although they weren't wearing his uniform. The tallest among them crashed into Sawyer's only other man in the office and the head of the mercenaries began to reach for his weapon.

One of the intruders covered the distance between the hole in the wall and Sawyer's position in three easy strides and Sawyer's right hand stopped on the butt of his weapon. The deep dark muzzle of a black blaster was less than three inches from his left eye and the man on the other side of it was grinning. "Not so fast, my friend."

More men were in the office now, the small room suddenly very crowded, and Sawyer lifted his hands into the air. "Get down on the rug very slowly and you won't get hurt," the man with the distinctly Soviet accent said and Sawyer complied. *Was Becker in league with the Russians?* He thought as he felt his hands roughly pinned behind his back and his weapon removed from the holster on his right hip.

Throughout the entire ordeal, Justin Calabrio had remained in his kneeling position in the center of the office. His eyes looked frightened and Sawyer laughed inwardly at the dark wet stain on the front of his pants. The man who was wearing the uniform of one of his team stood then and helped Becker to his feet. Removing the helmet from his head, Sawyer could see that this was not one of his soldiers.

"Aw, shit," he muttered and felt the muzzle of the blaster press a bit harder into the back of his neck.

"No talking from you," the Soviet accent said and Sawyer let his body relax. He wasn't about to die on the Moon today, not for the likes of that spineless Calabrio. Sometimes jobs went sour, this wasn't the first time and it wouldn't be the last, so Sawyer let all thoughts of fighting his way out of this exit his mind and he decided to ride it out to the end. He could always finagle his way out of this once the ordeal was over.

* * *

Tobias Thibodeau gave the custody of the mercenary he had tackled to Swayne Morrison and then stood to survey the office. Max was standing next to Becker, Dimitri was sitting atop the head mercenary, Martino had made sure that the office door was securely locked and Rider Boone had helped the young lady, whom none of them had expected to be here, to her shaky feet.

He made a slow circle to ensure that everything was under control and then turned to face the pathetic form of Justin Calabrio. He fixed the man with an angry glare and then turned toward Hans Becker. "Sir, you look a little rough, are you all right?"

"Yes, Tobias, yes, I'll be ok," the older man said in confusion. "What, what are you all doing here? What's happened?"

"We were able to create a little diversion, sir," Toby said and pointed a finger out the now glassless panes of the office. "My effects tech, I think you remember him, Ti Cho?"

Becker nodded and a grin appeared on his face.

"That's right, sir," Toby said. "He was able to gain access to the landing pad using your underground tunnel system and sabotage both of the shuttles in order to give us a little wiggle room once we got here. I'm sorry for the damage to your building and starport, Mr. Becker. It was…unexpected that the blasts would be so severe."

"That is quite alright, if it stopped this bastard's plans," Becker said and took one shaky step toward where Calabrio still knelt.

"So, you didn't sign the merger documents yet, then?" Max asked.

"No, I was just about to when that first shuttle blew," Becker said. "I had the pen in my hand, they had brought in Melanie and I...I..."

"It's ok, Mr. Becker," Toby said, noticing the facial bruising and bleeding lip of the young woman. "You acted accordingly, sir, especially under the circumstances."

"But, Toby, I still don't understand...I mean, you're the band, for goodness sakes!" Becker blurted.

"Yeah," Toby said and laughed. "That and a little more sometimes, Mr. Becker."

"The band?" Mick Sawyer said from his place on the rug. "The musicians?"

"Yeah, the musicians," Dimitri said and pressed the gun a bit harder into Sawyer's neck. "Now, shut the hell up."

"Max, why don't you rip up those documents," Toby said and Gun'jhur reached over to the desk to pick up the papers.

"Actually, Mr. Becker might enjoy that duty a bit more than I would, Tobias," Max said and Becker snatched the paperwork from Max's hands. Within seconds, the confetti-sized pieces fell to the carpeting of the office and Calabrio's jaw dropped open in wonder.

"You should feel amazed, Justin," Toby said and looked at Becker. "That is his name, right?"

"Yes," Becker said and fixed his attention on to the young man on his knees.

"Because, you see, you didn't just lose out on this deal today, Justin," Toby said. "I think you'll be surprised at all that's transpired this morning."

Just then a banging on the office door sounded and a gruff voice yelled from the other side to see if everything was alright. Toby motioned for Dimitri to let the leader of the mercenaries gain his feet and the tall musician addressed him directly. "Call off your forces, you don't work for Calabrio anymore."

"How's that, musician?" Sawyer said, having to tilt his head back to look up into the eyes of the tall man.

"Because…that man over there," Toby said and pointed toward Calabrio. "He's broke."

"What do you mean, broke?" Calabrio said, the first words he'd uttered since the band of musicians had stormed the office.

"I mean broke. Actually, broke and unemployed," Toby said. "As is your father and all of the other top-brass over at your organization."

"You are out of your mind!" Calabrio said. "My father's corporation is a multi-billion dollar operation."

"Hmmm, not anymore," Toby said and Max pulled out his MFM, handing it over to his boss. Toby fiddled with the controls for a few moments and then lowered the small screen so that Calabrio could see. "It seems that Becker Industrial Associates bought out your father's corporation just a little while ago. You see, it's all right there. All nice and legal. The documents have all been filed with the Universal Corporate Council, the money has been transferred over to Hans Becker's corporate accounts and the deal was sealed by both CEO's thumbprints. It's a done deal, Justin."

Calabrio slowly stood to his feet and reached his hands out to grasp the MFM. "No, it can't be! My father would not sell to him!"

"You're right," Toby said. "But it seems that there was a hostile takeover. It seems that you and your father have been beaten at your own game."

"You can't do this?" Calabrio muttered. "Who are you? You can't do this?"

"It's been done," Max said and shoved the little man back a step or two. "Sorry, that's how these things go sometimes."

"As for you," Toby said and motioned toward Sawyer. "He can't pay you anymore. If I were you, I would take whatever up-front payment that this little bastard gave you and run with it. If the transfer of money hasn't been secured, it could legally become a part of this transaction and you'll get nothing out of the deal."

"My boys and I don't take kindly to being cheated, musician," Sawyer said.

"You won't be, I'm sure that Mr. Becker here would be willing to pay you the remainder of your contract to ensure your cooperation in this matter. Maybe a bit more to ensure that you and your men won't come back to clean up a leftover mess."

"Absolutely," Becker said, his eyes also wide as he tried to discern this sudden turn of events.

Sawyer thought that over for a second and then nodded. "Done, I'll stand down my men."

"You can't do that!" Calabrio spat. "You work for me you imbecile!"

Sawyer laughed then and walked over to the little man. He grabbed him by the lapels of his expensive suit and hauled him to his tip-toes in order to bring the young Vice President a little closer to his face. "I don't work for you anymore, in fact, it seems that nobody does." With that, he let go of Justin Calabrio and spit in the thin man's face.

"Good day, gentlemen," Sawyer said and he glanced over at Max. "Is the man whose uniform you're wearing dead?"

"No," Max said. "He's in the Infirmary. Drugged."

"Very good," Sawyer said and looked back at Becker. "I'll be downstairs. When you finish here, sir, I'd appreciate it if we could finish our business as well."

"I'll be down soon, mercenary," Becker said with anger stewing behind his eyes.

"I know it's tough to give that man any money," Toby said as Sawyer exited the office. "But, believe me, it was nothing personal against you with he and his men. They work for whoever will pay them. He was acting on this little creep's orders."

"I know, Toby," Becker said and rubbed his bleeding and bruised face. "I know."

"The Universal Corporate Council might not approve the takeover if Calabrio decides to fight it with the Merger Committee," Toby said. "But, if you put enough pressure on the older Calabrio, especially in regards to leaking what has happened here today to the press and law enforcement agencies, he might back down and settle for a merger instead of an outright buyout. Something to think about."

"I'll consider it, Toby," Becker said and turned to hug his still crying secretary. Her sobbing grew to a crescendo as she fell into the arms of the older man, all of the stress and anxiety of the morning's events finally hitting home. Becker felt a few tears of his own stream down his face as he told her that everything would be ok now.

Toby handed the MFM back to Max and looked over the entire group. "Well done, guys," he said and let out a nervous laugh. "Dammit all to hell, well done!"

The tension in the room was gone then, in the blink of an eye, and all of them relaxed with the realization that the entire ordeal was over. Toby turned to Becker and shook the man's hand. "I wish we could have gotten here sooner, sir," he said, indicating the bruises and cuts on the older man's face.

"I still can't believe that you people did this at all," Hans Becker said and slumped down into his chair. "For goodness sakes, Toby, why? Why did you do this?"

Toby glanced at Max and smiled. The band's manager approached the head of Becker Industrial Associates and held out his micro-financial manager. The documents detailing Becker's hostile takeover of Calabrio Design & Manufacturing were gone from the small screen now, replaced by the payment screen for the band's performance last night.

"Well, sir," Max said and hesitated a moment before continuing. "We hadn't been paid yet for yesterday's show. If you remember, I had gone for my MFM just prior to that little idiot's arrival. And, well, we simply couldn't figure out any other way to collect our fee."

Becker laughed at that and clapped his hands together. "Astounding performance, both yesterday and today, my friends," He said and pressed his thumb to the spot indicated on the small screen. "In fact, double your fee right now and I'll affix my thumbprint to that screen, too."

Max looked over at Toby and received a nod in return. He made the proper adjustments on his MFM and Becker once again pressed his thumb against the screen. A small beep signaled the completion of the transaction and the musicians all smiled at their reward. "We'll be on our way now, Mr. Becker," Toby said and started for the door. "As for that little cretin, we can deliver him to your security office if you would like."

"No thank you, Toby," Becker said and turned to face the man. "I think I'll call his father so we can discuss this matter in further detail. But I would like several of my security men to be here when I do that."

Ti Cho entered the office from the outer corridor just then with a man in a Becker Industrial Associates Security Uniform and Toby sighed with relief at his Effects Tech's safe return. "Thank the good lord, Ti, we didn't know where you were," Toby said.

"I'd made it back down into the tunnel before triggering those charges but, man, did those shuttles ever go up!" Cho said and laughed. "Everyone here all right?"

"We are now," Max said, holding his MFM up high as the small group of musicians filed through the door of Hans Becker's office and into the corridor beyond.

Tobias Thibodeau had several things on his mind as he entered the ornate hallway—was there still enough time to make a shuttle hop down to Earth for the meeting with Fantasticon Productions? Would they be able to settle up quickly with the rental dealership on the destruction of the Valkyrie? Where might they be able to get their hands on some replacement equipment before the next gig? As he thought of these things and a few others during the first few steps he'd taken down the hall, something made him glance back at Hans Becker's office just as the heavy wooden door swung shut.

A moment or two later, Toby could have sworn that he'd heard several very heavy thuds followed by the painful high-pitched screams of the young Justin Calabrio still inside...

You Ain't Never Caught A Rabbit

The clinking of glasses, the soft murmur of dinner conversation and the sound of fine music, an old Italian opera, filled the surprisingly large space. The lights were turned dim and the many different smells of the various foods lying at the center of the large table brought back some very vivid memories, most of them good ones.

"Why so quiet, Tobias," Max Gun'jhur spoke lightly from his immediate right. "Aren't you enjoying this marvelous treat?"

Tobias Thibodeau allowed his eyes to roam over the Officer's Banquet Hall, settle on most of the faces, some he knew, some he'd just met, and then turned to face his business manager. "Of course, Max, I'm enjoying this evening very much. By the looks of things, you are, too."

Gun'jhur fixed him with a sly smile, raised a glass of deep red wine and clinked it lightly against Thibodeau's. "That's the spirit."

Suddenly there was the sound of a utensil being rapped quickly against a glass and all eyes turned toward the captain of the Rabbit II, seated to Thibodeau's left. "Quiet, quiet, everyone," the man said, looking regal in his dress blues, and fixed Thibodeau with a grin. "I would like to propose a toast. That is, if you don't mind, sir."

The man seated directly across the table from Thibodeau gave a short nod of his head and smiled. "Of course not, Captain Braithewaite, please do."

"Very good, sir," Braithewaite said, slid his chair back a few centimeters and stood. "It is with great honor that we dine here tonight along with the enormous musical talent of these very gifted people." Braithewaite paused for a slight round of applause. "It gives me great pleasure to know that I have sailed the currents of space with the lot of you, my new friends, and all of us here hope to do so again soon."

"Here, here," the man across the table from Thibodeau said and another small round of applause followed.

Braithewaite sat and reached over to lightly grab Thibodeau's arm. "You are an amazing musician, Mr. Thibodeau," the captain said. "One whose talents can not be known by those who merely listen to broadcasts of it. No, only those of us who've had the privilege to hear you perform in person can possibly know the enormous talent you possess."

"That's very kind of you, Captain Braithewaite," Thibodeau said. "But I'm just a player of music, nothing more."

"Spoken like a true gentleman," Captain Braithewaite said and leaned toward his employer. "What say you, Mr. Turney…are these mere musicians we dine with tonight?"

Glenn Turney shook his head from side to side and smiled, showing off his perfect white teeth. "From what I've heard so far, absolutely not, my friend, absolutely not."

Thibodeau bowed his head toward the white covered table and his now empty plate, feeling just a bit uncomfortable with the praise of this ship's owner and captain. Max saved him from the moment by leaning forward and catching the captain's eye. "My good Captain Braithewaite, this is one fine boat you have."

"It's not mine, Mr. Gun'jhur," Braithewaite said, although he swelled in pride at the compliment. "It belongs solely to Mr. Turney."

Max directed his attention to Glenn Turney and raised his glass. "Then to you, sir, a fine boat indeed."

"Actually, this is the second version of the Rabbit," Turney said. "The first one was lost in a rather unpleasant skirmish with border pirates along the fringes. All the crew was lost…I had this vessel built as an exact replica of the first and renamed it Rabbit II, in order to honor the men and women who had served aboard her predecessor. I was very lucky that day. Two minutes from boarding her for the journey before some business call or other begged me off the access ramp."

Thibodeau noticed Max stiffen at the mention of pirates, he was obviously recalling their own ordeal with piracy not too long ago. "Let's hope that this journey turns out differently, then."

Several people around the table laughed at that and Toby stood, looking toward Anita Salazar, three seats away. "Would you care to dance, Ms. Salazar?"

The band's back-up singer smiled, rose from her chair and took Thibodeau's proffered hand. Anita looked stunning in a low-cut blue satin dress, her dark shoulder-length hair and olive complexion a perfect contrast to the shimmering fabric. The dress fit snugly and Anita's well kept form had been turning heads all evening. As the two walked from the table to the dance floor, Thibodeau leaned down and whispered in her ear. "Thanks for saving me back there?"

"You were doing just fine, Toby," she said as they reached the floor and began a slow dance. "Why do you always get flustered around InterGridactic Trillionaires or military personnel?"

"It's a long story, Anita," Thibodeau laughed. He tried to avert his eyes from the generous amount of cleavage she was sporting tonight but, being at least a foot taller than she was, he was finding it very hard to do.

"Oh, please, Toby," she said and blushed. "I bet you've had this type of angle on female breasts your entire life…look at how tall you are, for crying out loud."

Thibodeau grinned at that and Anita stepped closer, pressing herself against him. "This is nice, Toby, we should get more gigs like this."

"You'll have to ask Max about that," Thibodeau said, catching his business manager in deep conversation with Glenn Turney and Captain Braithewaite as he and his dance partner twirled across the floor. A great chandelier hanging from the center of the magnificently sculpted ceiling was something to behold. The ornate dance floor was astounding, Thibodeau marveled at the work that must have gone into laying the millions of multi-colored tiles. The sheer scope of the project was truly mind-boggling.

He moved his left hand lower on Anita's hip and fastened his hold on her a bit tighter. He'd been enjoying her company very much so far on this trip. The great yacht was larger than most cruise-type vessels and there were many different great halls in which the band had entertained the various passengers these past few days. Usually unwilling to become romantically involved with anyone on the crew or in the band, Thibodeau was finding himself becoming more and more attracted to the dark haired beauty each and every moment he shared with her.

He looked down at her again only to find her looking up. Sharing a smile, they both looked at each other for the better part of a minute, lost in each other's gaze as they danced very slowly. "Boy, are you getting an eyeful tonight," Anita said and he somehow smiled wider than he'd been smiling, something that he wouldn't have thought possible.

"The view's great from up here, too."

"I just bet it is," she said, playfully kicking him in the shin.

"Hey, watch it now, don't go crippling the lead singer," Thibodeau chided just as the music suddenly stopped, only to be replaced by an announcement that reverberated off the walls of the enclosed space and seemed to echo inside Thibodeau's skull.

"Captain Braithewaite and Mr. Turney, your presence is required on the bridge," the voice sounded rushed and with a tinge of fear, Thibodeau thought. "Your urgent response would be greatly appreciated."

Thibodeau caught Anita's concerned glance and turned to watch as Braithewaite and Turney left the room in a rush. Max quickly approached from across the dance floor and Toby realized that Anita had not released his hand despite the fact that they'd stopped dancing.

"What is it, Max?" Thibodeau asked.

"They haven't a clue, Tobias," Gun'jhur said. "But I didn't like the tone of that message."

"Yeah, I caught that, too," Thibodeau said and squeezed Salazar's hand tightly.

"I knew this gig was too good to be true," Anita said and laid her head against Toby's right arm. Now there was a feeling he could learn to like, Thibodeau thought, then cursed himself for not staying focused on attempting to discover the cause of their newest apparent crisis.

*   *   *

Braithewaite entered the bridge followed closely behind by Turney. "My God, what could be so important…?"

"Sorry to disturb your dinner, Captain Braithewaite," the Rabbit II's First Officer said and gestured toward the viewscreen where an enormous ship was slowly rolling in space. "I thought that this was important enough to call you both here, though."

Braithewaite stepped closer to the viewscreen, taking in the gigantic size of the craft drifting lazily before them. "Reduce magnification."

"Sir, there is no magnification on that image," Percy Godwin said. "We came right in close to run the scans."

"You mean that thing's as big as it looks?" Braithewaite wondered aloud and Godwin nodded in affirmation.

"It's very large, sir," Godwin said. "I believe that it's the…"

"It's the Hound Dog," Turney said. "I recognize it."

Braithewaite turned toward Glenn Turney and raised his right eyebrow. "You mean Pressly's ship?"

"The very one," Turney said. "I've been on it a few times, I should know."

"Mr. Turney's correct, Captain," Godwin said. "We verified her identification by the markings on her hull, she's not transmitting anything. We couldn't even pry it out of her dead banks, sir. She's not giving up a thing."

"Any signs of life, Godwin?" Turney asked.

"No, sir."

Braithewaite let several silent seconds pass before he turned back to look at the image floating across the screen. "That ship must have been carrying at least ten thousand people."

"At the very least," Turney said. "She's so dark."

"Yes, sir," Godwin said. "Like I mentioned, she's a hulk. Simply floating. Who knows for how long."

"What could have happened?" Braithewaite asked.

"That's the strange thing, sir," Godwin said. "We've run scans on all sides of her, every nook and cranny. There aren't any signs of hull breach, no signs of any cataclysmic failure, nothing to indicate why she should be floating like that."

"Were you able to detect the bodies?" Turney asked.

"One more thing to add to the strange list, sir," Godwin said. "Our sensors didn't pick up anything in there. Nothing. It's as if all those people just left…all at once."

"What in the hell is going on?" Braithewaite asked. "This is impossible. With today's technology…what could it have been?"

Turney turned toward his Captain and sighed deeply. "Let's find out, those were good people. A competitor, no doubt, but very good people. That ship was Aaron Pressly's headquarters. He did all his business there. Those ten thousand people weren't merely passengers, they were his employees. They must have been headed somewhere for some purpose. Let's find that out and send a message to the nearest U.E.N. Outpost."

"Consider it done, Mr. Turney," Braithewaite said and began issuing orders to the bridge crew.

Turney took one last look at the vast floating hulk just outside his Rabbit's hull and felt a sudden sense of loss. Although he and Pressly had been fierce business rivals, the two had liked each other and often sought the other's company. Even when there wasn't any business to discuss. Not an actual friend but, Turney knew he would miss Pressly very much. Another sigh and he left the bridge to seek out his special guests. Perhaps they could play something impromptu and take his mind off of this horrible tragedy.

*   *   *

The band was sitting together at the same table when Turney entered the Officer's Banquet Hall. There were four musicians altogether, although he'd heard that their number sometimes grew to as many as ten or more. Add to that any number of crew and the band's manager, Gun'jhur, and that would make quite an entourage.

"My friends," Turney said, plopping down into the captain's chair at the head of the table. "Please accept my apology for my hasty retreat earlier. It seems that we have stumbled upon quite a tragedy and the bridge crew was correct in calling Captain Braithewaite and I away from dinner as they did."

"Oh no, what's happened?" Anita asked.

"We have found a very large vessel floating in space, a derelict it seems," Turney said. "Right now, there are no life signs."

"Do you know whose ship it is?" Thibodeau asked, noticing that Max had grown alert at the mention of a derelict ship, too. Especially in this lonesome and often dangerous portion of space.

"Yes, we do," Turney said. "It belongs to a competitor of mine. One of the major players in the InterGridactic market place. It's called the Hound Dog…"

"Aaron Pressly's ship," Thibodeau said. "His headquarters, if I'm not mistaken."

"Correct," Turney said. "You've heard of it?"

"We've played there many a time," Gun'jhur said, as if he were one of the musicians himself, and slumped softly in his seat. "Mr. Pressly was a great fan of Toby's and the band."

Turney smiled at that. "I'm sure he was. Pressly was a very musically oriented fellow, to say the least."

Thibodeau nodded at that. "I didn't know him very well, personally, but we enjoyed some very long conversations about the history of music, especially with that of the man he considered his namesake."

"The one he liked to call the 'King' of rock and roll," Turney said and smiled.

Thibodeau laughed and continued. "That's the one. We played for Pressly's employees at least twice an e-year. He had an enormous collection of music-related memorabilia. Most of it aboard the Hound Dog."

Turney laughed. "Of course, I should've known, that's where the tip to contact your Max here came from. It must've been old Pressly, it was sent to me anonymously."

Gun'jhur looked from Toby to Turney. "He'd mentioned to us several times that there was a business rival of his that would greatly enjoy our performances."

"Yes, it must have been him," Turney said. "I'll miss him, to be sure. I'd heard that his business affairs had fallen on very hard times recently, especially with some of his InterGridactic patents coming up for expiration. There'd even been rumors of a possible bankruptcy for all his business concerns. Times were growing dark for my old friend."

"Are you certain that he's dead, Mr. Turney?" one of the band members asked.

"Actually, no, not at this point," Turney said. "There are no life signs that our sensors can pick up but the ship is slowly rolling with no systems operational. No lights, no sound, no signals…it's dark."

Thibodeau shook his head in confusion. "This doesn't sound right," he said. "That ship must have held at least ten thousand people. Where are they?"

"We don't know, Mr. Thibodeau," Turney said. "But our sensors don't show any bodies floating around in that hulk either. It's very strange."

"A ghost ship?" Conor McCain, another of the musicians, asked and Max shot him a look.

"It might just be, young man," Turney said. "For all we know, they all simply blinked away. There's no signs of a hull breach, no signs of a critical systems failure. It's just floating, rolling actually and, from the looks of it, someone's turned it off."

"Can we get a look at it?" Thibodeau asked.

Turney turned a quizzical expression toward the tall band leader and said, "Well, yes, I suppose, if it will fulfill your sense of curiosity."

"Mr. Turney, you may not know this," Thibodeau started. "But all of us are very skilled engineers as well as musicians. It's one of the prerequisites for joining this band. We find that people who comprehend the intricacies of mathematics, the ebb and flow of higher math, understand music on a deeper level than most. It helps us to be better at what we do."

"Fascinating," Turney said and stood. "Then let's get you to the bridge for a look. If there's one thing we need, it's more points of view on what in the hell happened to Pressly's ship."

* * *

"There's no way around it, Mr. Turney," Thibodeau said. "We'll have to board the Hound Dog and find out what happened."

"That sounds dangerous, sir," Braithewaite said. "Perhaps our men should handle it. I'd feel better if men experienced in this sort of thing went over first."

"And how many men experienced in boarding gigantic derelict spacecraft do you happen to have in your crew, Captain Braithewaite?" Gun'jhur asked and the older man stiffened. "I mean that as no insult, sir, merely as a reference to the fact that none of you are actually experienced with what we have here."

"However," Thibodeau said. "We are."

"What do you mean, Toby?" Turney asked.

Thibodeau motioned toward Martino Velez and Conor McCain. "Those two are both former Engineer Corps, an exclusive group called on by the various branches of the U.E.N. Military whenever the need arises, and Conor there has even done some salvage work in his time. We've all been in a scrap or two in our travels and Max is an above-average pilot, too. At the very least, he could safely guide a small scout craft over to the Hound Dog and nestle it safely in a landing dock. First off, though, we have to stop that incessant rolling."

Braithewaite looked nervously from his boss to the band leader and back to Turney. "Well then, you seem to have the better of us in terms of actually boarding her. But you can leave the rolling issue to us."

"I'll come with you," Turney said to Thibodeau and Braithewaite snapped up from his chair. "Absolutely not, sir, I can not permit you to do so."

"Relax, Evan," Turney said. "The ship's been turned off, you said so yourself. We're just going to take a short ride over, check it out for ourselves and then we'll come right back. It's perfectly safe."

Braithewaite's eyes narrowed with concern. "Not without some of our own boys, sir. I must insist."

"Of course," Turney said. "I wouldn't have it any other way."

"We'll have to suit up," Martino said. "Do you have enough EV suits?"

"Yes," Braithewaite said after a moment's hesitation. "We have more than enough for a small party. But I still don't see why…"

"Don't worry, Evan," Turney said, raising a finger in an obvious signal to his ship's captain to be quiet. "What could go wrong?"

*   *   *

The small shuttle worked its way toward the landing deck in the belly of the Hound Dog and settled smoothly to the flat metal plates of the vast empty interior. The huge ship's rolling had been stopped moments earlier by an intricate series of tractor beams dispersed expertly by the Rabbit II's bridge crew. Thibodeau had been more than impressed with just how quickly their worst problem had been solved.

"Isn't it strange that the landing deck hatch seems to be missing?" Max Gun'jhur said and received several murmurs through the tiny speakers inside his helmet in return. "It's almost as if a hatch was never installed here."

"That's impossible," Martino Velez said. "Every ship has a landing deck hatch, especially one of this size."

"It's hugeness is impressive, isn't it?" Anita said. "But Max is right, I don't see a hatch or anywhere that looks like it could have rolled up into."

"We'll find one, it has to be there somewhere," Velez said as two of the Rabbit's crewman secured the docking clamps and opened the shuttle's exit hatch from their consoles in the tiny forward cockpit.

"Careful as you debark, people," a young voice sounded in Thibodeau's helmet. "We don't know what's going on here so be ready for surprises."

One by one, the eight suited figures emerged from the small hatchway and slowly floated to the deck plating, the magnetism in their boot soles ensuring contact with the metal surface. Everything was stark white, bright white, in the shuttle's exterior lights. But the total darkness lying just beyond the range of those lights made Thibodeau shiver inside his suit.

"I hate being exposed like this," Gun'jhur said, voicing Thibodeau's unspoken thoughts.

"Engage your suit lights," another commanding voice said and within seconds the interior of the vast landing deck grew far brighter.

"What's the plan?" Turney asked, his voice sounding smaller coming through the helmet speakers.

"We scout around, break up into two groups, keep in constant communications with each other and regroup here once the preliminary search is complete," Thibodeau offered.

"What exactly are we looking for?" again from Turney.

"Signs," Thibodeau said.

"Of what?" Anita asked.

"Of anything that can tell us what happened here," Gun'jhur finished and Thibodeau nodded.

"This ship is an anomaly," Toby said. "Some of us here have been on this ship before, it's usually bright, vibrant, almost alive with activity. Ten thousand people are usually aboard her during flights. Ten thousand. Where did they go? Why is this ship dead in the water, so to speak? Let's try to find out."

"Once again," Turney said. "What exactly are we looking for?"

"Anything unusual," Gun'jhur said. "Anything that stands out. Anything at all."

"Well I can think of one thing right now," Conor McCain offered. "This landing deck just doesn't feel right. I mean, from what I can see, it looks the same. But it doesn't feel right…you know what I mean?"

"It feels spooky to me," Martino Velez said and there were several grunts of agreement from the group.

"Conor's right," Thibodeau said. "It doesn't feel right. Something's wrong. Really wrong here. But, for the life of me, I can't put my finger on it."

"Conor and I will head down to the engine room, take a look-see," Velez said and Thibodeau nodded his helmeted head.

"I'll take Anita, Max and Mr. Turney to the bridge. One of the Rabbit II's crewmen should accompany each group," Thibodeau suggested and the crewmen nodded. "Each group should report their progress every five minutes. If one group fails to report, the other will work their way toward the last reported position of that group. Understood?"

More grunts of agreement and the eight figures made their way toward the landing deck airlock. Other than the beating of his heart and the quickened pace of his breathing, Thibodeau could hear no sound at all. The eerie silence was one of the things he hated most about extravehicular excursions into space. Although his suit was heated, he could feel the intense cold of space just inches away from his skin creeping into his bones. His fingers had gone ice cold and he could barely feel his toes. Deep down, he knew it was his mind playing tricks on him but the more steps he took into the interior of the vast empty ship, the more the urge to turn back and flee this awful place threatened to overwhelm his common sense.

"Let's get this over with as soon as possible," Thibodeau said to the group. "I won't be able to stand being here for much longer."

"I'm with you, boss," Max said as they reached the airlock door. One of the Rabbit II's crewmen brought a small device up to the entry access panel and entered a quick series of commands via the tiny keyboard. Thibodeau watched this all in complete silence and fought back the urge to look over his shoulder into the darkness that lay between the shuttle and their position.

The door didn't budge and the crewman repeated the process. When the door still didn't move, the man turned to look at Turney and Toby could see the man arch his eyebrows with confusion. "This should have worked, I don't understand."

"Let's see if the thing's even locked," Thibodeau suggested and the man placed both gloved hands against the large metal plank. With a minimum of effort, the hatch slid aside and a long empty corridor stared back at them. The interior was totally dark, a frightening blackness that Thibodeau was sure no one in the group wanted to be the first to enter.

"Jesus," Velez said and took one shaky step into the darkness. His suit lights played against the walls and the flooring, causing more shadows than there really were but Thibodeau gulped down the lump in his throat and followed his band mate into the murky depths ahead.

Soon all eight of them were in the cramped corridor, their suit lights bouncing off of smooth metal plating and leaving a good portion of the corridor still in an inky blackness.

"This still doesn't feel right," Thibodeau said out loud and felt Anita Salazar's suit bumping up against his from close behind. "Mr. Turney, you've been on this ship many more times than anyone else here. Can you tell me what you're feeling right now?"

Turney stepped through the group and took the forward position, allowing his suit lights to glance off the smooth metal walls. "I seem to remember carpeting here in this corridor and some piping running along the upper portion. I can't be certain but my memories of this corridor seem so clear. This is the only way out of the landing deck. Every time I've come here, I've had to wind my way through this corridor. As to why there aren't any pipes here, no carpeting...I can't say. Perhaps my memory serves me falsely."

"I don't think so," Thibodeau said as Turney's words brought it all together for him. "Mr. Turney's right. I remember this corridor, too. There was carpeting, a deep burgundy. There was piping, too, if you happened to notice it. Along with artwork adorning the walls and a handrail running along the left side. None of that here, though. In fact, I remember markings all over the deck plates in the landing deck, too. Do any of you remember seeing floor markings back there."

A few brief murmurs and it was established that none of them had. "Ok, so what we have here is a skeleton of the ship that we all remember," Turney said.

"Let's open one of these side hatches, take a look at another room," Velez offered and slid aside another unlocked metal panel. He poked his head into the room, allowed his suit lights to play around the bare walls and turned back to the group. "Empty and bare. No carpeting, no furniture, nothing."

"Where did it all go?" Turney asked. "Could the pirates who did this have looted the entire ship, taken everything of any value at all?"

"How many pirates do you know steal the carpeting off of corridor floors and take the time to dissolve the adhesive and scrape it all down to bare metal?" Thibodeau said.

"So what does it mean?" Anita asked.

Max and Tobias looked at each other through the clear faceplates in their helmets and both nodded in unison.

"This is a mock-up," Max said. "A dummy."

"Made to look, for all intents and purposes, like the Hound Dog but, in fact, just an empty hulk," Thibodeau said. "An elaborate look-alike, that's all."

"For God'sakes, why?" Turney asked.

"The hell if I know, Mr. Turney," Thibodeau said and turned toward the other end of the corridor. "I don't know about the rest of you but I've seen enough. Let's get back to the shuttle and report in to the Rabbit II."

Just then a crackle sounded in Thibodeau's helmet and an external link went live. "Attention Hound Dog boarding party, please return to the Rabbit II immediately."

"What is it, Rabbit II?" Turney asked.

"We have three ships approaching fast on long range scanners, sir, big ones," the voice came back. "And we've just picked up an energy source from the engine room of the Hound Dog. It's very hot and growing hotter."

"So is this a mock-up or what?" McCain asked as the group began shambling back down the corridor toward the landing deck.

"Rabbit II, does the energy source look like an engine signature, perhaps a warm-up cycle?" Thibodeau asked.

"Negative," came the immediate reply. "It's so hot, it screams of an incendiary. Reminds me of some of the military-grade explosives I've seen in action deep in my past. I have a nasty feeling about this and suggest that you make haste in your return."

"You heard the man," Turney said as the group attempted to hurry in the cramped confines of the corridor. "It sounds like this empty hulk is going to blow up soon and I want to be far from it when it does."

*   **

From the bridge of the Rabbit II, Max, Turney and Thibodeau watched the three blips signifying the three fast approaching ships. The rest of the band had gone to the science lab where the instrumentation there would allow them to better research the huge dead hulk floating just outside the hull. There were still too many unanswered questions, too much strangeness surrounding the ship.

"So, the question begs, why build a mock-up of one of the largest ships in the U.E.N. registry?" Max asked. "The only things I've seen larger than that floating hulk are military warships and those absurdly large cargo carriers. To build an empty framework on such a massive scale…for what purpose?"

"Good question, Mr. Gun'jhur," Turney said and bent over another monitor close by. "Those approaching ships are not running silent. They're still too far away for us to pick up any transponder activity but they're gaining fast. The fact that they haven't attempted communications yet can't mean anything good. They definitely know we're here, we're keeping no secret about it."

"I agree," Captain Braithewaite added. "This situation is about to get ugly. I suggest we power up and put some distance between ourselves and those three bogies."

"As well as that new mystery hot-spot on our free floating guest," Tobias added.

"Agreed, at full acceleration," Turney ordered and Thibodeau felt the slightest pressure of acceleration in the decking under his feet. Suddenly the dead hulk began to recede in the viewscreen, growing smaller as the Rabbit II scurried away.

"Captain," Godwin said from his post at another terminal. "I'm reading an increased energy reading coming from that hot-spot aboard the dummy Hound Dog. It's growing exponentially, perhaps triggered by a brief transmission we just detected originating from one of the three approaching ships. Whatever's going to happen will happen soon."

"Pour more speed into this rig, Godwin," Braithewaite said and his First Officer immediately relayed the orders to engineering.

"Hide your eyes!" Turney said as Thibodeau watched the viewscreen turn to bright white just before snapping his eyelids closed. The Rabbit II immediately began shaking and shuddering as the onslaught of energy waves created by the dummy Hound Dog's destruction pounded through space past their position. Thibodeau slowly opened his eyes now that the brightness on the other side of his lids had receded. A bright glowing central area, like the nexus of a galaxy seen from millions upon millions of miles, filled the viewscreen.

"What in the hell just happened?" Max said, rubbing his eyes with two fingers of his right hand.

"Our mock-up of the Hound Dog exploded it would seem," Braithewaite said as the bright remnants of the skeletal ship continued to grow smaller with the Rabbit's acceleration.

"The dummy began emitting transponder codes identifying itself as the Hound Dog about ten seconds before she blew," Godwin reported. "Along with a distress signal on all channels, multi-disbursement."

"What in the devil?" Max said but Thibodeau cut him short.

"Think about it, this all makes sense," the tall musician said. "Whoever's behind this has created an elaborate plan to hijack the

Hound Dog and kidnap the Senior Officers of Aaron Pressly's business conglomerate. They built the dummy Hound Dog, took over the real ship, spirited it away from here and left the dummy with an explosive device aboard obviously strong enough to reduce the entire ship to very tiny pieces. All they needed was the mock-up so that any investigation into the matter would find small bits of a ship resembling Pressly's headquarters vessel. The transponder activity and distress call was a brilliant move, it'll make the authorities think that the ship ran into some fatal problems and blew up quickly, killing everyone aboard."

"Still, why?" Turney asked. "And why are those three ships still approaching?"

"My guess is they were part of the force that kidnapped Mr. Pressly and hijacked the real Hound Dog," Max offered. "They must have noticed us on one of their last scans and turned around to see how much we were able to learn during our recent boarding mission. When they saw just how close we were to the dummy Hound Dog, they must have grown suspicious that we'd uncovered the truth behind the mock-up. Then they poured on the speed and raced toward us."

"So, now we are chased by these same marauders," Braithewaite said and grinned. "Good then, let them come."

Turney turned to face him and returned the smile. "Thinking what I'm thinking, Evan?"

"What's going on here, you two?" Max asked and Turney laughed once.

"When the first Rabbit was…lost, I swore that her replacement would never fall into that kind of trap again. I've built the Rabbit II with faster engines and with an accompaniment of various weaponry the likes that no corporate yacht has ever seen."

"Careful, Mr. Turney," Thibodeau warned. "We have no idea who is chasing us, what their armaments are or how fast they are. You wouldn't want to test the Rabbit II's new toys against such a mystery."

"Why wouldn't I, Toby?" Turney asked. "How better to discover if I've gotten my money's worth?"

* * *

Aaron Pressly fidgeted in the captain's chair aboard his Excalibur Class Yacht, Blue Christmas. The captain of the boat stood mere inches away, standing at attention, no doubt resenting Pressly for usurping his command chair at this moment of crisis.

The plan had been brilliant, he was sure that it couldn't have been foiled by anyone, even by an experienced investigator in the U.E.N.'s SpaceBorne Emergency Response Unit. But then…disaster! Turney, damn him! His competitor's yacht had turned up at the most inopportune time! Minutes, they were just minutes away from destroying the Hound-Dog Doppelganger and all would have been made right in the universe.

His numerous business entities had experienced a major financial collapse over the past several months. His inner investigative unit showed massive errors and poor management as the primary culprit though Pressly knew that his idiot son was responsible. Three e-years ago he had been stupid enough to let the boy take over most of the figurehead duties that he himself used to perform, allowing the desire for more vacation time and a life away from the hell that was everyday business to cloud his better judgment. The kid hadn't been ready, had never understood the big picture of Pressly's corporate mission, and had begun to make horrible decisions behind his father's back.

Now, here he was, ready to turn tail, fake his own death and ride off into the proverbial sunset as a fugitive from justice. The plan should have worked, it should have been pulled off flawlessly…all except for Turney. Glenn Turney, bitter rival, sometime friend. A man he simultaneously detested and held a deep fondness for had come here and laid waste to all his grandiose plans for a re-birth. Over the past week, Pressly had dissolved most of his secondary businesses, allowing them to be taken over for enormous sums of cash by lesser competitors.

All under a sworn secrecy and with the stipulation that most of his employees would continue on at their positions under the supervision of their new employers.

All of this had been done very quietly during dozens upon dozens of secret meetings with some no-face legal outfits who specialized in such shady dealings. None of it was legal but, who would care? At the end of the investigation, all of InterGridactic Space would think him dead and the building blocks that had been put in place over the past week would make it seem to the U.E.N. authorities that the smaller businesses owned by Pressly were being sold off to counteract the uncountable amount of debt currently owed by Pressly Enterprises.

It was a win-win situation…none could lose. His employees would continue working, his business entities would be absorbed by his rivals, his debts would be covered by the subsequent liquidation of his main business holdings and his death would be reported in all four Corporate Grid-Sectors. He would be mourned by trillions, he would watch the various stories of his life, some kind, some no doubt cruel, blaze across the nets and laugh and cry along with everyone else.

That is, if he could stop Turney from finding out the truth. There was no doubt the scoundrel had figured out the falsehood that was the Hound Dog's doppelganger. Especially if their scans were true and a small landing party had made it aboard before the ship blew.

Once they had appeared within scanner range of the Rabbit II and Turney's ship had turned around to run…Pressly knew the decision he would have to make. Thus far, his grand scheme had cost nobody their lives. But, in order to ensure that his good name not be smeared in the history books with tales of shady business practices, deals gone bad and shoddy management, he would have to destroy the Rabbit II and everyone aboard her.

How ironic, Pressly thought to himself, *that the original Rabbit had been destroyed just a few e-years ago during an unwelcome visit by pirates.* Everyone aboard had been killed…all except Turney, who had been called off the ship at the very last moment by an unexpected problem that needed his utmost attention. Pressly had been foiled back then, too. Those pirates had failed to establish concrete proof that Turney was aboard the Rabbit that day. If Turney could have been killed back then, when Pressly's business woes had first begun to show themselves, perhaps some of his troubles would have gone away due to the turmoil that would have overtaken Turney's various business interests.

Oh well…Pressly knew, to cry about what could have happened, should have happened, would have happened was to waste your tears and your time. Here he was right now, at the tail end of what should have been his glorious ride off into the sunset with his dignity intact and his InterGridactic reputation gone to the grave. Instead, he was giving chase to Glenn Turney, trying to outrace the Rabbit II and put an end to the threat that now hung over his grand plan like a great and dark menacing cloud.

"Can't you push this boat any faster?" Pressly snarled and the captain's head swiveled quickly around to stare down at him.

"We are at our maximum speed, Mr. Pressly," the tall and emotionless face of Captain Curry stated. "And we are gaining on the Rabbit II. We should be within weapon's range in mere minutes. Would you wish to deliver the fire-order, sir?"

Pressly bit his lower lip, cursed himself for being a sentimental fool and hesitating just this very tiny bit before issuing his answer. "Of course, captain. Let me know at the very soonest when we are in range. Perhaps my skeletal Hound Dog's destruction couldn't catch this Rabbit, but this ship's long-range missiles should be up to the task."

"Of course, Mr. Pressly," Curry said and turned his face back toward the viewscreen. Pressly knew that the captain of this lead ship thought him an old fool, as did the captains of all the other ships in his fleet, including the real Hound Dog, which was making due time toward the fringes of the U.E.N. / U.S.S. Border at this very moment.

"Screw you all..." Pressly muttered under his breath and noticed just a flicker of movement near the eyes of tall Captain Curry. "It's my money that makes you listen to this old fool and it's my money that will make you all continue to do so."

"Excuse me, sir?" Curry said without turning to face Pressly this time.

"I said, you ain't never caught a rabbit before today, Curry," Pressly snapped. "But, right here and right now, is your chance to show me that you're worthy of wearing those stripes on your sleeve."

"Have no worries, Mr. Pressly," Curry said in a snide tone that Pressly wasn't sure he liked very much. "By now the Rabbit II knows who we are, we've been in transponder range for quite some time. He'll see that his ship is more than outmatched and he'll accept his defeat. Mr. Turney's Rabbit will stop her running soon. Mark my words."

"Screw your words, Curry," Pressly said and slumped back in the captain's chair. "Just catch her already and let's turn around. My retirement and fake death have waited long enough already. Let's do this deed and be done with it."

Curry laughed once, a slight yet impetuous snort. Pressly knew the sound for what it was. The response of a man who hated his boss yet tolerated the old man's presence as long as it meant that more money kept flowing into those unmarked accounts. Part of the plan, part of the scheme and part of what made Pressly's overwhelming influence among his employees so complete.

*   *   *

Conor McCain and Anita Salazar entered the bridge aboard the Rabbit II with a pile of flimsies in their hands. "Wait til you see what we found on old Aaron Pressly."

"What do you mean?" Turney asked and grabbed the flimsies from McCain's hands.

"Take a look for yourself, Mr. Turney," Salazar said as she nestled up close to Thibodeau's left arm. "We were able to hack our way into his corporate network, raid his files and find some juicy tidbits on just how badly Pressly's financial outlook has become."

"These are incredible," Turney muttered, handing the sheets he was finished with to Thibodeau who then handed them to Max. "Simply incredible."

"Good work," Thibodeau said as he scanned the flimsies. "Now I guess we know a bit more about why the mock-up ship was constructed and what Pressly's plans were for the immediate future."

"Was he really in this bad a shape?" Turney asked as he scanned the numbers, all the horrible negative numbers. "Could Pressly Enterprises have been this bad off?"

"If Pressly's own files are to be believed," McCain said. "Martino is still working on more of this stuff. We thought it best to update you with what we've found so far, though."

"I'm glad that you did," Turney said and fixed Max Gun'jhur with an angry glare. "So this is why he's chasing us, then. Because he has to silence us, everyone on this ship, in order for his scheme to work. With us free to spoil the announcement of his supposedly fake death, he will not be able to pull this off."

"It seems very likely to me, Mr. Turney," Thibodeau said and glanced worriedly back at the console showing the three ships consistently gaining ground on the Rabbit II. "We know that he means business now. This information also identifies those three ships as the fastest and most heavily armed in his fleet. We know that Pressly most likely means to cause this ship's destruction. Is there any reason to give him the chance to fulfill his wishes?"

"I find it hard to believe that a man I was playing chess with mere months ago would now hunt me down and kill everyone aboard my ship just to guard his most ugly secret," Turney said and raised a single finger when Max looked ready to retort. "But this information, stolen from Pressly's own databanks, is most convincing. You and your people have done their part, Toby. For that, I am very grateful. With your assistance, we were able to board that ghastly mock-up, that soulless ghost of a ship, and learn the secrets behind Pressly's master plan. For that knowledge, the man now hunts my ship. Perhaps planning her destruction. But, before I can bring myself to do harm to those three vessels, I must see proof of these dark intentions myself. I can not rely on words and numbers. You must understand."

Thibodeau nodded his head slowly up and down and turned toward Max. "Mr. Turney knows his ship's capabilities. He knows what it can and can not do. If he thinks he can match up against the Blue Christmas, the Lonely Street and the Cellblock, three of Pressly's strongest vessels, then who are we to argue?"

Max began to protest but found himself staring at another raised finger. "Max, I can see it in Mr. Turney's eyes. He has a confidence in this ship that comes with knowledge about its capabilities that we do not have. I say, let him see this through. It's his ship."

"Jesus, Toby," Anita said and gave a short laugh. "I know he hasn't paid us for this gig yet but...this is ridiculous."

"I don't think so," Thibodeau said and turned to face Turney. "I think the owner of this Rabbit has a trick or two up his sleeve."

* * *

Curry grabbed a hold of the cushioned backing of his captain's chair as the ship accelerated at speeds that were in the red on the engine's specs. Dammit if they shouldn't have already run the Rabbit II dry by now but the little ship just kept going. It would slow, allow them to gain, and then accelerate again against all possibility. It was very frustrating to say the least but the threats to be done with this thing had continued to spew forth from Aaron Pressly's mouth, goading him on, making him push his ship harder, to the limit.

The old bastard was really being a son-of-a-bitch now, right here at the apparent end of the chase, and Curry was more than determined to shut the old fool up, collect his vast riches and escort Pressly into deep space before starting his own life over again on some resort world with enough money to retire comfortably on.

If only the Rabbit II's engines would give out already, the smaller ship just shouldn't have been able to run this long. "Tyler, what's the range?"

"Captain, the range to Rabbit II has not changed since the last time you asked," his First Officer snapped. "Still too far away for our missiles to be effective."

"You're sure that they've identified us, Curry?" Pressly wheezed.

"Yes, sir, they know who we are," Curry said quickly, annoyed at the distraction. "We've made no secret of our identity due to our confidence that we'd be through with them shortly. You might want to hail them, sir, ask them why they're running when you only want to talk."

Pressly darted an evil look toward Curry, stung by the words. Curry knew full well that the old man would not be able to look his former friend in the eye and then nonchalantly order his execution. "Just get closer, you fool, and we won't have to. What's wrong with this ship? Where does all my money go to? You told me that we could catch them…a long time ago, I might remind you."

"We'll catch them, sir," Curry said and absentmindedly wiped a bead of sweat from his right temple. "We'll catch them just as…"

"Sir, the Rabbit II has initiated communications," a voice called from a console behind the captain's chair.

"Patch it through," Curry said and glanced over to see Pressly stiffen. Suddenly the scene of space and the small outline of the Rabbit II disappeared. In its place was Glenn Turney's face.

"Aaron? What's the meaning of this? Why are you chasing us?" Turney asked, the dreadful look on his face made Pressly turn away.

At the uncomfortable pause that was created by Pressly's reaction, Curry responded. "You should know by now the purpose of this chase, Mr. Turney. Surely you could not have risen to such a successful position if you were not able to figure this out."

"I want to hear it from Aaron Pressly himself if you don't mind, you second rate excuse for a ship's captain," Turney snarled.

"Turney," Pressly rasped. "That's a hell of a way to talk to your killer. You have no hope, why don't you just cut engines and let this happen nice and quick so I can go on back and enjoy the rest of my life in peace?"

"So it's true, then," Turney stated. "You aim to destroy this vessel…just as you ordered the original Rabbit destroyed?"

* * *

Pressly gasped and felt his heart tighten in his chest. How had the man found out? How had he known?

"No need to answer, Aaron," Turney said. "I see the truth on your face. I just wanted to make sure for myself before I sent you to an early death."

Curry laughed at that and managed to speak through the rage that had threatened to overwhelm him upon Turney's insult. "Your meager ship has no hope against these three vessels, Turney. You are clearly overmatched."

"Quite so, it would seem, when looking at the schematics of a normal example of a ship of this class," Turney said. "But need I remind you that several of my subsidiaries specialize in military weapons development, warship upgrades and engineering design?"

Pressly felt his heart skip a beat, then another, and his breath was starting to come in slow raspy gasps.

"Oh, please, Aaron, don't die just yet," Turney said. "I want to have the pleasure of killing you myself. That's the least of my vengeance, you murderous bastard! When you ordered the destruction of the Rabbit, you didn't kill me as planned, but you managed to murder a thousand of my best and brightest employees. People who counted on me to protect them. People whose families are without fathers, mothers, sons and daughters because you wanted to save your petty little empire. A pathetic fool you are to say the least, Aaron."

"Kill him," Pressly whispered as his red-lined and rheumy eyes settled on those of Glenn Turney. "Kill him, Curry! Kill him!"

"They are still out of range," Curry spat.

"Oh, are we?" Turney asked. "Let's fix that."

Suddenly the Rabbit II decelerated so rapidly that all three of Pressly's ships shot past unable to react quickly enough to the daring move. As Pressly, Curry and the crew of the Blue Christmas panicked on the bridge, trying in vain to turn their ship around or target their weapons systems on the Rabbit II, several very small objects were jettisoned from Turney's ship, accelerated at great speed toward Pressly's little armada and simultaneously made contact with their hulls.

Pressly felt a moment of great heat as his eyes were blinded by the purest white light he had ever seen just before his world went black.

* * *

On the bridge of the Rabbit II, Tobias Thibodeau removed the hand that was covering his eyes from the glare that had filled the viewscreen a moment before. The destruction of all three of Pressly's ships, all of them large, within a millisecond of each other had caused the large screen to be overwhelmed before the auto-glare reduction could kick in, immediately causing it to turn itself off.

Now the screen snapped back on, showing an instant of black and white fuzz, before resuming its view of the scene directly ahead of the Rabbit II. Bits and pieces of the three ships that had been chasing them were twirling in space, spitting bits of fire out into the vast background of stars. Turney's ship had accelerated rapidly backwards when the ships had been destroyed, putting some much needed distance between them and the ensuing explosions. Still, the tiny pings of metal bits could be heard bouncing off of the hull immediately outside the bridge. Thibodeau looked up at the sound with a worried glance and Turney laughed. "Don't worry, Toby, that trash won't penetrate this hull."

"You seem confident of that," Anita said.

Turning toward Salazar, Turney touched her hand lightly and said, "I am."

In his right fist, Glenn Turney held the final bit of information that had brought him to the unfortunate decision he'd just made. Two minutes prior to putting in the call to Pressly's Blue Christmas, Martino Velez, one of the musicians, had burst on to the bridge with a new set of flimsies. The one on top detailed the deal that Pressly had made with the pirate ship to destroy the original Rabbit a few e-years ago. In full detail, ripped from the heavily guarded electronic files of Aaron Pressly himself. Velez had run the information to the bridge and Turney had gasped.

Since the destruction of the Rabbit, Turney had visited Pressly several times aboard the Hound Dog. Had played various games of skill with the man, had held many a conversation with him about the current state of InterGridactic business and where the U.E.N. economy was headed over the next decade.

He had become better friends with him, had thought himself a member of Pressly's inner circle, had thought that the two of them were closer than mere business competitors. But that single flimsy had brought to him such a rage, a complete and utter hatred of Pressly and what his three ships signified.

Of course, there was no reason to suspect that Pressly knew of the Rabbit II's upgrades or new weapons technology. No reason to believe that Pressly had any fear whatsoever of the fleeing Rabbit II.

The old man's confidence had betrayed him and now Aaron Pressly was no more. Turney sighed at the memory of the man who he had thought a friend and handed the flimsies back to Velez. "Take these, please," Turney said. "I've seen what they hold and would live my life out very peacefully if I never lay eyes on them again."

"Of course, Mr. Turney," Velez said and shot a questioning glance at Thibodeau. Tobias nodded and Velez took a step back, allowing Thibodeau to move in closer to the Rabbit II's owner.

"This is one amazing ship, sir," Thibodeau said, breaking the awkward silence aboard the overcrowded bridge. "I don't even think I felt the slightest bit of pressure when she decelerated so rapidly before."

"That's because she's been redesigned with…" Braithewaite started but Turney held up a hand for silence.

"No need to bother with small talk, my friends," Turney said. "I just ordered the deaths of many people on those three ships. Not just that bastard Pressly. Of course, we really had no choice. They were going to destroy us, Pressly as much as admitted that."

"He even ordered his captain to kill us," Max said. "I heard him say it. You had no choice."

Turney paused and a small smile came to his lips as he looked at Maximillian Gun'jhur. "I know that, Max. Believe me, I know."

"You will need to report this to the nearest U.E.N. Outpost, Mr. Turney," Thibodeau said. "We'll all make official statements of what transpired here today. We'll also make ourselves available if you need witnesses through any future…proceedings."

"Thank you, very much for that," Turney said. "And for digging up that awful information. I don't know how you were able to do it from here, this ship, so small in the overall scheme of things. But I do thank you. Now I can finally report the facts to the families of all those employees killed when the original Rabbit was destroyed. That incident has played havoc on my emotions these past several e-years, of that there is no doubt."

"It was no problem, sir," Velez said and Turney nodded toward him.

"Actually, I don't know how effective our testimony will be for you, Mr. Turney," Max said. "We might be considered by the courts as valued witnesses since we don't actually work for you or any of your business entities but, then again, we were in your employ during this trip which might taint our testimony as biased."

"It makes no matter," Turney said. "All that transpired during our discussion, Pressly and I, was recorded in this ship's computers. Pressly's admission that he was chasing us to our supposed deaths. His orders to Captain Curry to kill us…or me, I should say. All was recorded. There will be no need for a formal inquiry or for even the merest of legal proceedings. Especially with the information that you researched on what happened to the original Rabbit. I might even be invited to a share in the vast Pressly wealth as compensation. A nice healthy share, to be sure."

"At least you have closure now, Mr. Turney," Thibodeau said. "Some of us aren't ever so lucky. The truth can sometimes work wonders."

"Such wisdom from a musician," Turney said and laughed. "And for Pete's sake, my name is Glenn."

"All right then, Glenn," Thibodeau said and took Turney by the arm. "I may be a musician, one with just a tiny bit of wisdom, but my lecturing is over for today. How about we all go back down to the Officer's Banquet Hall and my band mates and I will play a short set all for you. At no extra charge."

Turney laughed again and raised a hand to Thibodeau's high shoulder. "Charge me all you like, Tobias, with what you and your people did for me today…I've decided to triple your fee. Press me a bit more on the matter and I'll quadruple it. Agree not to play anything by Aaron Pressly's favorite musician, the one whose songs all of Aaron's ships were named after, and I might just quintuple it."

Thibodeau stopped short, glanced at the smiling members of his band scattered about the bridge, looked back down at Turney and stuck out his right hand. "Glenn, my friend, you've made our little group happier than you'll ever know. Let's shake on it, you've got yourself a deal."

A Little Less Conversation

"So that's it, Max," Red Alonzo said from the other side of a small table in the bar at the base next door. "Is that all of it?"

"Not nearly, Ms. Alonzo," Max said, swirling the beer in his hand. "That's just some of it, just enough to give you something to start with."

"It's Red, Max," Alonzo said and Max nodded his acknowledgement as she took a sip of her beer. The music was soft and there were people dancing in the middle of the bar, some still in uniform but others in civilian attire. "And what do you mean by just enough? How much more could there possibly be to tell?"

Max suddenly got a far off look in his eye and his smile wavered a bit, just for a moment, before his eyes sparked up again and he turned his beaming smile toward Red. "There's more…but that's for another time."

"So, there's going to be another time?"

"If I played my cards right," Max said and chuckled. "But, for now, a little less conversation, a little bit more action, please…"

With those words, Max reached for Red's hand and led her to the dance floor. The other members of the band, sitting at a booth in the far back corner of the bar all smiled and raised their drinks to their Manager and his charms.

Red smiled and couldn't believe how this unforgettable day had gone. First an attempt at a jailbreak in the middle of a concert, then learning of the multiple adventures that this particular band had been through during their history and…now… now… dancing with the enchanting Max Ghun'Jur, manager to The Player…and having more Excitement in one day than she'd ever thought possible.

Pulling Max closer to her as they danced, she whispered in his ear, "Yes, a little more action, please…"